"I'm in a bind," Ari admitted grimly.

"I may have somehow given Social Services the impression that you live with me, and now that I've expressed an interest in adopting Lucinda, they want to come out and interview us together in my house."

Cleo stared back at him with parted lips of dismay. "How on earth could you have given them the impression that we live together?"

"I think the lady simply assumed that when you came with me to see the baby the first time that we were a couple—"

"But we're not," Cleo cut in sharp as a knife.

"That's not to say that we couldn't be," Ari sliced back at her with determination. "I will do literally *anything* to be considered as my niece's adoptive parent. If that means doing whatever I have to do to gain your willing participation, I *will* do it."

The Stefanos Legacy

The billionaire's vow to reunite his family!

When his father dies, renowned Greek tycoon
Aristaeus Stefanos is devastated. Not only at the
loss of his beloved father, but also at the shocking
discovery that his father had feet of clay—in the
form of two secret daughters!

Ari will do anything to track down his half sisters
and offer them his protection—his sense of honor
demands nothing less. But his priorities are turned
upside down when it's revealed he also has an
orphaned baby niece. Ari must put his quest to
find his long-lost family on hold to focus on the
tiny infant who needs him—and on finding the
bride he needs to claim his niece!

Read on in
Promoted to the Greek's Wife

The thrilling first book in *USA TODAY* bestselling
author Lynne Graham's sparkling new trilogy!

Lynne Graham

PROMOTED TO THE GREEK'S WIFE

Recycling programs
for this product may
not exist in your area.

ISBN-13: 978-1-335-56834-2

Promoted to the Greek's Wife

Copyright © 2022 by Lynne Graham

This edition published by arrangement with Harlequin Books S.A.

For questions and comments about the quality of this book,
please contact us at CustomerService@Harlequin.com.

Harlequin Enterprises ULC
22 Adelaide St. West, 41st Floor
Toronto, Ontario M5H 4E3, Canada
www.Harlequin.com

Printed in U.S.A.

Lynne Graham was born in Northern Ireland and has been a keen romance reader since her teens. She is very happily married to an understanding husband who has learned to cook since she started to write! Her five children keep her on her toes. She has a very large dog who knocks everything over, a very small terrier who barks a lot and two cats. When time allows, Lynne is a keen gardener.

CHAPTER ONE

'FORGET ABOUT THEM,' the family lawyer had advised. 'Should a problem arise in the future, provision has been made. Your inheritance is ring-fenced. There is no reason why you should concern yourself with this issue.'

Even today at the newly opened London HQ of Stefanos Enterprises, where the proof of his own exhilarating rise to success should have put him in a very different mood, Aristaeus Stefanos couldn't get that unscrupulous little speech out of his head. Only a month had passed since his father's death. A renowned philanthropist and business mogul, Christophe Stefanos had been a much-admired figure. A loving son, Ari had been devastated by his sudden death, and in all the years he had known his father, he had never once doubted his essential decency.

In retrospect, that complete trust now struck him as ludicrously naive for a male of twenty-eight years of age. Death had, after all, cruelly exposed his parent's darkest secret and had shattered Ari's faith in him. Ari had been forced to acknowledge his father's feet of clay and to make a decision that he might some day regret even while accepting that he could not *live* with any other option. Fierce conflicting emotions still bubbled uneasily beneath Ari's controlled surface. Angry shame and disbelief still rose uppermost whenever he reflected on his father's choices.

Life, however, was too short to agonise over what could not be changed, Ari reflected grimly. For that reason, rather than taking advantage of the many social invitations that had come his way since his return from his father's memorial service in Greece, he had decided to do something he had never done before: get to know some of his employees. It wasn't Ari's style to get close to his workers. A billionaire shipping tycoon and resort developer, he hired professionals to monitor his staff and kept his distance. His need for a distraction, however, had won out, and what could be more of a diversion than his participation in a company retreat to be staged in the wilds of Norfolk?

The new HQ of Stefanos Enterprises brought staff together from several different sites, and his HR director had suggested the retreat as a means of bringing down barriers and improving communication. Ari wasn't quite sure he believed in the value of company retreats. He understood the concept and the potential benefits, but he also suspected that many of his executive staff would view the retreat as a nice little holiday on company time.

His handsome mouth quirking, Ari left his office just as an eruption of giggles sounded from the reception area. His hard, dark gaze arrowed in that direction, and exasperation flooded him at the sight of a security guard flirting with the receptionist, who irritated the hell out of him. What was her name again? Cleo, he recalled, and even the name was inappropriate for a female with a mop of blonde curls and blue eyes. Cleo, short for Cleopatra, was, in Ari's highly experienced opinion, the name for a tall, dark beauty, *not* an undersized one with the curves of a pocket Venus and the dress sense of an eighties swagged and ruffled floral curtain.

It was fair to say that Ari had no time at all for Cleo the temp. But then she had blundered badly on her first day by letting Ari's stalker-type ex, Galina Ivanova, walk into his office unchallenged. Of course, she had apologised. *Thee mou*—had she apologised! While Ari never used two words if one would suffice, Cleo was a hopeless chatterbox and capable of utilising fifty words to do the work of two. She had apologised to him for five solid minutes, staring pleadingly at him with those huge blue eyes of hers that made her look more like a cherub than a grown woman. Having been made aware by Human Resources that he could not simply sack her out of hand, he had grudgingly accepted the apology, but her presence in his vicinity offended him.

'Have a nice afternoon, Mr Stefanos!' Cleo called cheerfully, not having the wit to pull a low profile after being caught in the act of distracting the security guard from his job.

Ari struggled not to respond with something derisive and told himself off for letting so minor an incident darken his mood. But Ari liked absolutely everything in his life shipshape and *tidy*. He had placed things in neat little groups since he was a child. Back then he had found security in making and restoring order. The testing times of his childhood were unforgotten, although he chose not to dwell on them. His wardrobe was colour-coded, his bookshelves alphabetically arranged, his desk immaculate. In his world, there was no clutter and everything and everybody had a place. When anything was out of place, it set Ari's teeth on edge, which was exactly why the receptionist irritated him, he reasoned in exasperation.

Cleo didn't 'fit' Stefanos Enterprises. She lacked dress sense and sophistication. She was too visible, too chatty and too friendly. She smiled too much. Spend five minutes in a taxi rank with Cleo and she would divulge her entire life story without the smallest encouragement. That kind of verbal licence gave Ari the chills. Thrusting her from mind, he reminded himself that he had a Norfolk-bound helicopter waiting for him...

Cleo clambered into the minibus with her overnight bag.

A lot of the staff were travelling to the retreat by car, but she hadn't made any close friends at Stefanos Enterprises and she hadn't been offered a lift. People rarely made much effort to get to know temporary employees and she was accustomed to being somewhat invisible at work when others were socialising. Even so, she had been thrilled to be included in the retreat, which was probably because she would be working at Stefanos Enterprises for another eight months.

She suppressed a grimace, thinking of the incident on her first day that she suspected had ruined any hope she had of ever stepping into a permanent position at Stefanos Enterprises. An enviably confident sleek dark beauty, dressed to the nines in designer fashion, had approached Reception to announce that she was lunching with Mr Stefanos and would go straight through to his office. Cleo hadn't even thought of questioning the woman further. She had simply assumed that the woman was a regular visitor, possibly even a family member. She hadn't been shown the banned list of visitors before she began her shift. She hadn't been told that the boss's lovers never had access to him during working hours either by phone or by personal appearance. And nobody had been more shaken than her when she saw the furious woman escorted off the premises by two security guards and one of his personal assistants came running to ask what on earth had she been thinking when she had allowed that 'madwoman' into Mr Stefanos's office. An ex, a stalker-type ex, apparently, who refused to take no for an answer and kept on showing up in the hope that he would change his mind. Cleo felt that she should have been warned the minute she took over the desk that her employer's adventurous, ever-changing love life included such a deceptive personality.

Cleo suppressed her unproductive thoughts. She preferred to concentrate on positive things. A night away from the cramped little studio apartment she shared would be very welcome. Although she had been grateful to find city accommodation that she could share, she often longed for the peace and quiet of her own space, but with the cost of rents in London and her less-than-stellar earning power, that was a luxury she could only dream about. In any case, she reminded herself, she was lucky enough that her landlady, Ella, spent a couple of nights a week at her boyfriend's place, leaving Cleo in sole possession of the mezzanine bedroom space and the tiny living area they had to share. Ella's parents had bought the property for their daughter and it really wasn't large enough for two people. Ella, however, was a student, who was struggling to get by, and she needed Cleo's rent.

The retreat was being held at a boutique country hotel, situated deep in the countryside and surrounded by woods and fields. The bus arrived late, after an accident caused a long, slow tailback of traffic. As they waited for their key cards at Reception, several remarking on the fact that their belated arrival excluded them from joining the team chats, Lily, one of the clerical staff, turned her head to say to Cleo, 'Come on… You're sharing with me.'

Cleo forced a smile, able to see that her companion was no keener on the arrangement than she was. No sooner had they arrived in the comfortable hotel room than Lily was excusing herself to join her friends. 'We'll be in the bar after dinner… You're welcome to join us,' the pretty blonde told her with a pleasant smile. 'The more the merrier.'

And a strange face was easier tolerated in a

crowd, Cleo reflected ruefully. She was pleased about the invitation, just a little worried that she would not truly be welcome and was only being asked out of politeness. 'I'm going downstairs to see what I can sign up for.'

'The yoga classes are supposed to be very good,' Lily informed her on the way out of the door. 'And they've got one on first thing...'

Cleo wasn't fond of yoga. Having once signally flopped at twisting her body into a pretzel shape at a class and having felt an absolute failure, she had decided that she simply wasn't bendy enough.

After freshening up, she went downstairs to explore the other options on offer. Breathing in deep and mustering her courage, she signed up for paintballing and stand-up paddleboarding the following day. Although she was not remotely athletic, she was a firm believer in moving out of her comfort zone when the opportunity was presented, and goodness knew, she thought ruefully, she was unlikely ever to receive another opportunity to try out such activities free of charge. At the very least, it should be fun.

Throwing herself in head first was Cleo's way when she felt intimidated. Growing up with a single mother perpetually fretting and expecting disaster had taught her to be fearless. Lisa Brown had always had a pessimistic outlook, while Cleo preferred to look on the brighter side of things.

Getting changed for dinner, she tugged out a stretchy comfy dress and heels. The bright colours of the jungle-palm print made her smile, whisking her back to her childhood with a mother who habitually wore black, believing that colours were less elegant. A lot of good that dark, colourless wardrobe had done her poor mother, Cleo reflected wryly. The man she loved, Cleo's father, hadn't loved Lisa Brown back and hadn't wanted a child with her either. Lisa's pregnancy had eventually concluded their clandestine relationship.

Cleo went down for dinner, glancing round the dining room and seeing only a handful of vaguely familiar faces. She was keeping an eye out for Ari Stefanos, who was reputedly joining his staff for the retreat. That had surprised her, Ari not being the most approachable of employers, and true to form, Lily had mentioned that he was not staying in the hotel, but in some separate luxury property in the woods, well away from the hoi polloi. No, Cleo was looking out for Ari simply because it was always a treat to feast her eyes on him. Those cheekbones, that unruly blue-black hair, that piercing dark-as-night gaze set below level ebony brows, not to mention the lush pink of his eminently kissable mouth.

The first time Cleo had met her employer had been the same day she had attempted to tender an apology for the woman she had allowed to walk unchallenged into his office. That had been her first glimpse of him, and sheer fascination had mesmerised her because there was just something about the precise arrangement of his perfect features that had made her stare like an enraptured schoolgirl. Her tongue had tripped over words, her mouth had dried up and her brain had closed down in that same moment. Ari Stefanos exuded irresistible appeal with every breath that he drew.

He was Cleo's secret addiction. It was a harmless piece of fun. All the women in the office treated Ari Stefanos to more than one glance: he was shockingly good-looking and smboulderingly sexy. He cast ordinary men in very deep shade. But he was a safe target for appreciation because his distaste for office flings was incorporated in her employment contract. In any case, Cleo knew that she didn't have the looks to attract such a man.

Cleo had never been in love and had no desire to fall in love either. Her mother had loved her father and it had ruined the best years of her life. No, Cleo would only allow herself to fall in love with a man when it was clear that *he* was keen enough on *her* to make a commitment. That was where her mother had gone wrong, trusting promises made in the heat of the moment, making the assumption that deep feelings were involved when they were not. Cleo had no plans to make the same mistake.

And in the short term, admiring Ari Stefanos from a safe distance was an amusing, perfectly prudent and private source of enjoyment.

Unaware that anyone received entertainment simply by looking at him, Ari led a discussion on the company vision for the future before heading for the bar, determined to have one drink and be sociable before he retired to his own quarters.

For some inexplicable reason, his attention immediately landed on Cleo and stayed locked to her. She was seated with a group, engaged in animated discussion, her mop of golden curls glinting in the low lights as she moved her head. She stood up to walk to the bar and he almost winced at the sight of the vivid giant-palm-leaf print she was sporting. A large blue butterfly was stretched across her curvy behind and, like the leaf cupping her full breasts, the loud design somehow accentuated the lush fullness of her glorious curves. In that instant he understood perfectly why she continually attracted his notice. She might be barely over five foot, but she had a superb figure. Pretty good legs too, he noted absently, watching her at the bar, catching her gurgling laugh and the brilliance of her smile as the bartender surged to serve her.

'She's very pretty and very young,' his senior PA, Mel, commented at his elbow as she looked in the same direction.

Ari tore his gaze from Cleo, faint colour edging his high cheekbones as he registered the throb at his groin, and shifted uneasily. 'She talks too much.'

'Yes, but she's very good on Reception,' Mel countered. 'Friendly, helpful, welcoming. In my opinion, she's a big improvement on that frozen fashion doll out on maternity leave.'

Ari gritted his even white teeth. 'She dresses badly.'

Mel frowned and gave him a surprised look. 'So, let someone give her the advice to tone down the colours a little and look more...er...professional.'

Tiring of the conversation, Ari tipped back the whisky brought to him without savouring the vintage. 'I'm going to turn in now. It's been a long day.'

Cleo didn't spend the whole evening with Lily and her pals, just an hour to be friendly. She went to bed smothering a yawn, wondering where Ari Stefanos had disappeared to, because she hadn't seen him. She woke and went down to breakfast alone because Lily had gone to the yoga class. Clad in a long-sleeved top and cargo pants, she ate and then followed the signs to the wooded, fenced area that held the paintball operation. She was a little embarrassed to see that only one other woman had chosen the activity and she was an athletic former soldier, whom Cleo had met the night before in the bar, and she was jogging on the spot with eagerness. Cleo put on her mask, helmet and protective vest and grasped the gun after it had been demonstrated for her benefit, and then she tried to strike a fit pose as if she too were fizzing with pent-up energy.

Ari Stefanos strode into view with a small group of other men. His black hair was tousled and in need of a cut. Cleo curved back into the shadow of the wall the better to watch him before he disappeared into the equipment shed. She wondered what it was about those features of his that continually locked her attention to him. The dark deep-set eyes, the rawly masculine hard jawline and faint shadow of stubble? The thin aristocratic nose? That beautiful mouth, which she had never seen smile? With the recent death of his father, she supposed he didn't feel he had much to smile about. He was very tall, spectacularly well built, all lean muscle from his wide, strong shoulders, flat stomach and narrow waist to his long, powerful legs.

The group was split into two teams and the game began. Cleo was ambushed behind a tree when she was least expecting it. Three of her own team, young and boisterous types, cornered her and literally sprayed her with paintballs, laughing uproariously as they did it. As the balls struck and spattered over her, she was startled by the force of each hit and by how much it hurt. She cried, 'Stop it!' as she felt the stings of pain and the pressure that would surely bruise her, but they were still laughing hysterically as they ran off again.

When they were gone, Cleo was left in a rage. Her own team members had attacked her, presumably because she was a temp, a safer target for a prank than a permanent staff member and an easy mark! And she was hurt, aching all over from the assault as she began clumsily picking herself up again, furious tears blinding her.

'You're out… Take yourself off to the dead zone,' a curt voice instructed.

'I'm not out! My own team ambushed me!'

'Got witnesses? If not, you're out,' the voice told her without sympathy.

'I'm going to get my own back,' Cleo countered furiously, recalling how turning her back on unkind behaviour aimed at her at school hadn't won her any favours. When anyone deliberately set out to injure Cleo, she had learned to always fight her corner in self-defence. It didn't pay to let people walk over her. If she allowed such treatment, it would be more likely to reoccur.

'That's against the rules. Neither is that attitude in the spirit of proper gamesmanship,' her unwanted companion informed her in a lofty tone of superiority.

'Oh, shut up!' Cleo said sharply. 'If they can ignore the rules and attack me, I can do it back!'

Below Ari's disbelieving gaze, Cleo shimmied up the tree behind her like a miniature ninja warrior. 'They won't even see me up here. I'm going to get them!' she hissed.

'Did you listen to anything I said?' Ari enquired drily. 'Did you even read the rules? You're not supposed to climb the trees or attack from above. Once you're hit, you're out and you should leave the field immediately.'

'A lot of good it did me reading the rules when nobody else is following them!' Cleo shot back, unimpressed. 'Go away and leave me alone. You'll draw attention to me and that'll wreck my plan.'

'Get down and I will see you get off the field safely,' Ari breathed impatiently.

'Like I need your help!' Cleo snapped. 'Anyone ever told you to mind your own business?' Reaching up to a higher, sturdier branch, she clutched the gun awkwardly below one arm. 'I'm about to teach those guys a lesson!'

Ari had never had an employee simply ignore his commands before. Undoubtedly, the helmet and the mask were a better disguise than he had appreciated. Ari was a stickler for rules, and while he understood her burning desire for retribution, he could not condone it. Stretching up, he closed his hands around her small waist, and from that angle, he really could not avoid noticing that in the close-fitting pants her derrière jutted out like a particularly ripe and luscious peach. Disconcerted by the instant swell of arousal against his zip, he tugged her down from the tree and brought her carefully down to ground level again. Of course, he knew who she was. Cleo was unique amongst the top-floor staff. She was too tiny to be mistaken for anyone else.

'What are you *doing*?' She gasped in disbelief.

As she staggered, he bent down to steady her and the faint scent of strawberries emanated from the golden hair curling out from beneath her helmet: he was too *close*. Ari took a sharp and deeply conservative step back from her as he spun her round to face him. The cornflower depth of blue that distinguished her eyes was distinctive. He tensed while he censured himself for his overt physical reaction.

'I'm taking you out of here,' Ari told her curtly. '*Before* I lose my temper with you.'

'Just because you have a different take on how to play games—'

'Breaking the rules could lead to the game being stopped for everyone,' Ari warned her curtly. 'There are safety concerns here. Please…'

And it was his accent, roughening the edges of his vowel sounds with a growl that made her steal a longer frowning glance at him. In one fell swoop she rose above her rage sufficiently to recognise the clothes that he wore and the dark golden eyes flaring like a shower of sparks behind the mask. *Oh. My. Word.* She was fighting with the boss, the great rule upholder!

'I'm so sorry, Mr Stefanos,' she murmured flatly. 'I didn't realise it was you.'

'Maybe I should have worn a warning label,' Ari riposted as he retained a controlling hand on her shoulder and steered her towards the boundary fence and the area marked out for the paint-spattered losers.

As the first arrival in the losers' corner, Cleo gritted her teeth on a snarky reply and compressed her lips, saying stiffly, 'Thank you. I'll head back to the hotel to change.'

Ari leant down to her level from his great height. 'I promise you… I'll cover those bullies in paint!' he murmured fiercely.

'Don't exert yourself on my account, Mr Stefanos,' Cleo remarked thinly as she walked away. 'After all, it's only a game...'

Ari snatched in a sudden sustaining breath, incredulous at her insouciant gall, and he stood there for several taut seconds watching her disappear from view, defiance in every line of her shapely, sexy body. The natural sway of her hips stole his masculine attention. He gritted his teeth and swung away, furious at the fact that she evoked a visceral sexual response from him. She was an employee. Such a reaction was unacceptable.

Still furious, Cleo stomped back to the hotel and straight into the shower, unhappy until she had rinsed the last speck of paint from her body. Faint pink circles of bruising marked her arms, her neck, her legs and stomach. It was her own fault for not wearing thicker clothing and for not taking advantage of the extra protective gear on offer in the equipment shed out of a fear of looking naff. Now she was suffering from an attitude adjustment and a growing retrospective horror about her unfortunate encounter with Ari Stefanos.

Talk about a clash of opinions! She shouldn't have been arguing with anyone in the game, considering that she was the most junior member of staff on the retreat. She couldn't afford to foolishly offend anyone higher up the ladder than she was...

and what had she done? Only attracted the wrong kind of attention to herself *again* with the boss! She winced as she donned her swimsuit and got dressed again. Ironically, she was no longer in the right mood to try out a paddleboard following her unfortunate experience with the paintballing. But Ari Stefanos was truly the most infuriating guy! So bossy, so confident and bold in his conviction that only his way was the right way and, while Cleo had never considered herself a rule-breaker, his strictures had made her madder than a hornet.

In the end she decided the encounter didn't much matter in the scheme of things because she had probably already given him the very worst possible impression of herself and her talents on her very first day at work. No point crying over spilt milk, she told herself firmly, reminding herself that at least nobody else had witnessed their exchange of words.

Consoled by that reflection, she went downstairs to an obligatory first-aid class and accompanied Lily's group into lunch. Everyone talked about what a beautiful day it was to go out on the lake. Cleo's spirits lifted when one of the women insisted that you didn't need to be especially fit to succeed at paddleboarding. Words like 'slow' and 'peaceful' increased her optimism as she clambered awkwardly into a wetsuit in the changing rooms. They all helped each other do up the back zips and there was much laughter as they added the life jackets and compared their bulky images.

Ari almost smiled when he saw Cleo walking down to the edge of the lake with her friends. There was nothing sexy about Cleo in her current apparel. Indeed, Ari felt wondrously safe looking at her, and he told himself that he had imagined his former response to her. The instructor stood on the wooden pier to see everyone safely disposed onto their boards. Cleo stepped onto the board like someone stepping onto hot coals, an oddly frozen expression on her face as though she was forcing herself to do something she didn't want to do.

As she used the oar to push away from the pier, it caught on something, jerked and fell from her hand, and she immediately lurched off balance. For a split second, Ari glimpsed the sheer terror on her face, and then he was instinctively moving forward because the instructor had already moved away while he adjusted someone's life jacket for them. Cleo plunged face first into the water with a tremendous splash and scrabbled frantically for the board. Ari recognised the pure panic in her reaction and the ineptness of her flailing hands. The board was right beside her, but she seemed to be too alarmed actually to see it. Someone was laughing, but Ari had already seen more than enough. He dropped down into the water beside her and grabbed her, lifting her above the water with easy strength.

'Relax, the water is barely a couple of metres deep at this point—'

'I'm not a couple of metres tall!' Cleo gasped, spitting out lake water in disgust. 'I'll drown at that depth—'

'No swimmer could drown in water this shallow,' Ari informed her forcefully, capturing her flailing hands. 'And calm down... You're not in any danger—'

'I *can't* swim!' Cleo hissed in a desperate undertone. 'I know I've got the jacket on and I'm sorry, but I'm very nervous—'

Ari dealt her an arrested appraisal. He lifted her up onto the side of the pier and hauled himself bodily up beside her. 'You can't swim? You actually went out on the water without being able to swim?' he demanded in a rising crescendo of incredulity.

'I've got a life jacket on,' Cleo protested.

'Have you a death wish? The minute you hit the water you panicked! Have you any idea how many people drown because they panic?' he raked down at her wrathfully.

'I wasn't likely to drown unless someone deliberately held me down under the water!' Cleo slung back at him in furious denial. 'And while you may not be my biggest fan, I doubt if you were about to do that—'

'You're an absolute bloody idiot and you should stay away from water!' Ari flamed back at her, dark eyes brilliant with anger, kissable mouth hard as granite. 'What you did was stupidly dangerous!'

Alerted by his wrathful volume, every eye in their vicinity had now turned to them, and Cleo cringed. She was shivering with cold and the after-math of fright. Ari Stefanos was standing over her in a rage and it was too much to be borne in the mood she was in. Cleo swallowed the lump in her throat, but her stricken eyes still flooded with tears of hurt and mortification.

A woman broke the horrible silence in which everyone on shore had fallen quiet and hurried forward to wrap a large towel round Cleo. 'Let me take you back to the hotel,' she urged. 'You've had a shock.'

'Thank you, Mel,' Ari breathed in a compressed undertone. 'But I'll take care of Cleo.'

CHAPTER TWO

CLEO SCRAMBLED AWKWARDLY upright and, because she felt shaky, she removed the life jacket very slowly while breathing in deep.

'Let me help you… You're swaying,' Ari murmured, scooping her up into his arms and striding away from the pier before she could object to his high-handed behaviour.

'I'll be fine when I get back to my room,' Cleo insisted tightly, shivering within the damp towel and closing her eyes to envision a blissfully warm shower and privacy. 'But I hate you…'

Ari released his breath on an audible hiss because he was well aware that he had screwed up. 'I kind of hate me too at this moment.'

Eyes wide with surprise, Cleo turned her head to really look at him as he settled her down into the front seat of an open-topped buggy. 'You disrespected me… You humiliated me,' she condemned thinly.

'It was an overreaction and I apologise. I saw my twin sister drown when I was a child. It…er… upsets me when people take risks in the water, but I shouldn't have taken that out on you,' he breathed, taking a split-second decision to drive on past the hotel sooner than face the challenge of escorting a wet, distressed and tear-stained woman through a busy reception area.

Cleo was stunned by that very private admission. Curiosity had made her look him up on the internet and that information about his sister had not appeared in his history. Of course, what she had read had related to his education, his business prowess and his sex life, which had been encyclopaedically covered. All his exes had struck her as being of a particular type: tall glitzy brunettes, socialites and models, spiced with the occasional up-and-coming actress.

Scolding herself for her wandering thoughts, she concentrated instead on what he had just told her. Naturally, he would have been traumatised by the experience of seeing a sibling drown, and even she, who didn't like him, could begin to understand and forgive what he had termed an overreaction. For the first time she recognised that Ari Stefanos, the gorgeous, wildly successful billionaire, was not omnipotent and, indeed, was as human and prone to errors of judgement as she could be.

Ari shot the buggy to a halt outside an opulent two-storeyed and balconied wooden cabin surrounded by trees and got out. 'Come on. You'll feel better once you have a shower and warm up—'

'But why did you bring me here instead of back to the hotel?' Cleo demanded, climbing out of the buggy at a much slower pace, an uncertain look on her heart-shaped face.

'It's more private.' Ari raked lean brown fingers through his wind-tousled black hair in a gesture of frustration and gave her a rueful look. 'You were crying. The hotel is very public.'

'I'm not crying any more. It was just a momentary thing…caused by shock,' Cleo pointed out defensively. She squelched up the steps to the front door and, in embarrassment, kicked her sodden footwear off to leave it outside before she stepped indoors barefoot.

'There's a shower through here,' he told her, pushing open a door.

'You didn't think this through, did you?' Cleo said uncomfortably. 'I have no clothes to change into and I'll need a hand to get out of the wetsuit.'

'Trivial,' Ari pronounced, tugging her forward and turning her round to attack the back zip of the wetsuit. 'I'll have our clothes brought here.'

He unzipped the suit, blunt fingertips grazing the smooth, soft skin of her back, and she shivered, shockingly aware of him. She tugged loose her locker key and spun round to hand it to him.

The confines of the bathroom suddenly seemed very small and tight, and breathing felt like a challenge when she glanced up uneasily to meet the lustrous dark gold of his black-lashed gaze. Those ridiculously lush long black lashes of his had gold tips, she thought crazily, locked there in stillness.

'I suppose I should ask you to perform the same service for me,' Ari murmured.

'I suppose…unless you're a natural contortionist,' Cleo mumbled thickly through her dry mouth, ducking her head to move behind him and stand on tiptoe to reach the zip on the back of his suit. Every brain cell in her head felt as though it had died as a long slice of golden satin-smooth brown back showed through the parted edges.

Cleo backed off to the side and tugged at the sleeve of her suit to start removing it, reminding herself that she was wearing a perfectly respectable swimsuit underneath. Yet she was feeling as awkward as a woman forced to perform a strip in public.

Catching a glimpse of Cleo's full rounded breasts cupped in smooth, stretchy material, her movements accentuating the luscious depth of her cleavage as she struggled with the sleeve, was not to be recommended, Ari decided when he went as hard as a rock, every libidinous instinct sparking instantaneously. In an effort to distract himself, he reached for the edge of her sleeve and gave it a sharp yank, enabling her to get one arm free.

'Thanks,' she said, warm colour blossoming in her cheeks as she began peeling her other arm free of the flexible fabric.

His wetsuit hung down round his waist, exposing a flawless bronzed masculine torso and the lean muscular perfection of sculpted abs and pecs. In her haste to draw back and put some space between them, she almost collided with him.

'Not enough room in here for the two of us,' Ari pointed out jerkily, backing away in turn to step back into the hallway. 'I'll sort out the clothes and leave them outside the door for you.'

'Th-thanks,' she heard herself stammer while still staring at him as if he had dropped down in front of her from the moon.

Her palms were sweating, her skin had come out in goosebumps and she was running out of oxygen. He was beautiful, like a glossy picture in a book and just as unreal and untouchable. An odd clenching sensation thrummed between her thighs and she knew what it was—oh, yes, she knew what it was, and it was absolutely *not* anything she should be feeling around her employer. Her face burned hotter than ever.

'Can you get out of that suit alone?' Ari pressed in a roughened undertone.

'Yes, of course,' Cleo declared, hurriedly shutting the door, turning the lock, flinching in even deeper embarrassment when it made a noisy click.

But that instant when she had recognised just how powerfully she was attracted to Ari Stefanos had thrown her back in time to her first love, Dominic, and that could only send chills through her. She didn't want to feel like that again about anyone! Dominic hadn't been her boss or a colleague, though, just a salesman who came into the office occasionally. She had fallen for him like a ton of bricks, although with hindsight she reckoned it had only been an infatuation. He had been young, good-looking and full of easy banter. There had been nothing suspicious about him and, as far as was possible for her, she had checked him out before deciding to commit to their relationship and sleep with him. He would have become her first lover had his girlfriend not turned up on her doorstep clutching their toddler.

To be fair, Imogen hadn't been nasty. She had just said, 'Dominic does this… He gets bored with us and strays… But he always comes back again. It's not your fault. He tells lies and he's very convincing, but he will get bored with you too.'

And Cleo had realised to her horror that she had

almost fallen into the same trap as her mother. Her mother had only been a convenient outlet for her father, who had also had another woman in his life. Cleo had been badly burned by the experience she had had with Dominic. The fear that she might place her trust unwisely in a man haunted her whenever she dated and made her very wary.

Irritated by thoughts of her less-than-successful dating past, Cleo managed to remove the wetsuit and her swimsuit and rummage for towels on the open shelves before she stepped into the shower.

The warm water combatted the shivers running through her. She shampooed her hair, thinking that she shouldn't be feeling guilty when nothing had happened between her and Ari. Attraction was normal, but people didn't always act on it, and in any case, she doubted very much that he was equally attracted to her. She had seen the sleek, expensively dressed and giraffe-legged females he dated on the internet, women with the kind of beauty that she had never had. On a good day in her very best clothes and all done up, she could shoot at being pretty, but she wasn't distinctive or particularly sexy, and she didn't have classic features.

He had classic features and yet that description severely understated the ability of his features to linger inside her head. She always wanted to stare at him, to linger with pleasure on the full curve of his lower lip, the clean-cut perfection of his angular jaw, the blue-black luxuriance of his hair and his spectacularly noticeable eyes.

Such reflections were ridiculously immature and foolish, she conceded as a knock sounded on the door and Ari informed her that her clothes had arrived. She wondered how he had achieved that miracle at such speed and she reckoned that it was probably something to do with the fact that he was very, very rich and people seemed to fall over themselves in their eagerness to please the very, very rich.

Wrapped in a towel, she opened the door and ducked back inside with her bag, quickly pulling on her jeans and long-sleeved top, regretting that she had worn her supposedly waterproof shoes down to the lake because now she had nothing else for her feet. Without her miracle styling spray that suppressed frizz, she would also have to leave her hair to dry naturally.

Cleo emerged into the silent hall and went straight for the front door to leave, but it was locked and the key had been removed. Rolling her eyes in frustration, she walked quietly down the hall into the large sitting room and sat down on a comfortable sofa to await the reappearance of her careless host. A wave of tiredness engulfed her because she hadn't slept well the night before with Lily just across the room from her engaged in constant texting with her boyfriend.

Ari strode downstairs, his black hair still damp from the shower, and stared in surprise at Cleo, who was curled up in a ball on the sofa fast asleep. He studied her, struggling to identify what it was about her that roused his libido to such an extent. She wasn't his style, and yet when she had turned those big blue eyes on him, lust had roared through him in a surge of heat that had left him thunderstruck. He breathed in slow and deep, steadying himself. Of course, that urge was not something he would ever succumb to, he reasoned confidently.

Ari was as organised and restrained in his sex life as he was in everything else. He had a select band of willing lovers in his life with whom he spent occasional casual nights and he had never had an exclusive relationship. Sex was a release from tension, a sporadic pastime, something enjoyable rather than exciting. Perhaps that was the secret of Cleo's appeal, he mused. She excited him and he could not recall when a woman had last had that effect on him. Possibly actual excitement in that field had evaded him since he'd left the adolescent years behind.

Wry amusement tilted his mobile lips. He was

well aware that he was spoiled in the female department, never being asked for anything more than he was willing to give because women wanted him to continue to call. He received endless invitations and selected only the most tempting from women he viewed as 'suitable'. Cleo wasn't and never would be suitable, he conceded calmly.

He was hungry. He swept up the phone and glanced at Cleo's tumbled mop of guinea-gold curls over the back of the sofa. He would order dinner for her as well, make up for his outburst down by the lake by being sociable with an employee for a change. He was very much a loner, he acknowledged. But then he had been an only child born to two only children, so there never had been much of a family circle to enjoy, which was naturally why the family lawyer's revelations had been so very intriguing.

Ari viewed his slumbering guest with amusement. There was something impossibly sweet about that innocent lack of intent. Women never fell asleep in Ari's radius because they were invariably keen to utilise every possible moment to impress him. Certainly, he could not imagine any other woman he had ever met cheerfully telling him that she hated him, as Cleo had done without hesitation. She was outspoken, again not a quality he was accustomed to because people were not honest around him, not if there was the smallest risk that that honesty could offend or indicate anything that could prove to be personally prejudicial. Cleo didn't guard her tongue or pay lip service to his position even as her employer.

As she shifted and stretched like a little cat in wakefulness, Ari leant over the sofa to say quietly, 'I'm ordering dinner—'

'Ah!' Cleo squealed and shot off the sofa and upright, huge blue eyes locking to him in consternation. 'You gave me a fright!'

'My apologies… What would you like for dinner? Or should I ask what would you *not* like?'

'Dinner?' Cleo gasped, backing away in apparent dismay, wide blue eyes pinned to him as though he were a ghost.

Ari was hugely entertained. 'I'll just order for you,' he decided, lifting the phone to contact Reception and order steak with all the trimmings for two.

'Why would you offer me dinner?' Cleo framed as he replaced the phone again.

Ari gave her a slanting smile that unleashed butterflies in her already tense tummy. 'I don't know. Do you think it could be an attempt to make amends for being rude to you?'

'That's not necessary, Mr Stefanos,' Cleo declared woodenly, her discomfiture unconcealed as she contemplated her bare toes digging into the plush luxury rug beneath her feet.

'I think it is,' Ari asserted. 'So, sit back down and relax…'

He had to be joking on that front, Cleo thought, incredulous at the idea of sharing a meal with a billionaire, who was also her boss. Even so, if he was trying to be nice when he was so obviously *not* a nice person on her terms, it would be mean of her to deny him the opportunity. Grudgingly, she sat down very stiffly in an armchair.

'You've had a pretty rotten day of it,' Ari pointed out quietly, determined not to smile at his recollections. 'You got ambushed at the paint-balling and you fell in the lake when you tried to go paddleboarding.'

Stony-faced at those unwelcome reminders of her lack of athletic talent and physical grace, Cleo nodded. 'I'm not an outdoorsy person, but I like to give things a go—'

'That's an admirable trait,' Ari remarked, thinking that she was about as 'outdoorsy' as an exotic plant plunged into the frost, but he was impressed that she had been willing to try.

'Except when it comes to activities in the water,' she dared to remind him of his opinion.

'I may be in a minority, but I did think that your participation in those circumstances was dangerous and, worst of all, the experience gave you one hell of a fright,' Ari told her drily, letting her know that he hadn't changed his opinion of her daring in the slightest. 'Would you like a glass of wine?'

'Thank you.' Cleo nodded again and tucked her restless hands between her thighs because she had never been more conscious of a man's scrutiny. Those dark golden eyes that lit up his lean, darkly handsome features held her fast as glue.

Cleo watched him uncork a bottle of red wine and fill glasses, his every move smooth and dexterous, his polished assurance as much of a draw as his devastating good looks. Cleo had never met a male that confident and there was something oddly reassuring about that quality. 'I suppose I should have panicked when I found the front door locked,' she confided abruptly.

Ari glanced back at her with a raised brow of enquiry.

'Locked in a house with a strange man…' Cleo clarified in a belated attack of mortification because she could see that that aspect had not once crossed his mind. And why would it have? she asked herself ruefully. Women rarely wanted to escape from young, rich and very handsome men.

'I'm sorry. It didn't occur to me that you would wish to leave immediately,' Ari countered, walking away from her and back to the door to replace the key that he had removed in an act of personal security that came to him as naturally as breathing. 'There, it is possible for you to leave now whenever you like…'

In receipt of that demonstrative response, Cleo had turned as red as a ripe tomato while secretly cursing his decision to take her word so literally. She took a strong glug of her wine.

'Is the wine okay?'

'I don't drink much, so I don't have an opinion to offer,' Cleo admitted tautly.

'I thought everyone in your age group indulged,' Ari remarked.

'I don't like the feeling of being out of control. I remember my mother…' Just as she voiced those words, her lips compressed. 'Sorry, you don't want to hear about that—'

Ari elevated a brow, deciding that yanking Cleo out of her shell could take more effort than he was capable of awarding her. For all her bubbly friendliness on Reception and her surprising backbone and defiance in adversity, she was amazingly shy. Clearly, only fear of losing her employment had turned her into a chittering chatterbox in his office the day they had first met.

'I do. I'm trying to get to know you. Did your mother have a problem with alcohol?' Ari prompted with deliberate boldness.

Cleo paled, shrugged. 'Only for a while, when I was younger and I didn't really understand what had happened. She had broken up with my father and obviously she was upset for a time because she knew she wouldn't see him again.'

Ari angled suddenly intent eyes on her troubled face. 'You grew up without your father?'

'Yes. He had a relationship with my mother, but not with me.' Cleo winced.

'And how did that work?' Ari Stefanos asked her with apparent interest, his entire focus on her, which was a rather unnerving experience.

Indeed, the sudden intensity of those black-lashed burnished bronze eyes of his was mesmerising and her skin broke out in goosebumps of awareness. She shifted uneasily in her seat, mortified by her reaction to him.

'I can't see how you would be interested in that,' Cleo commented edgily, not knowing a polite way of telling him that the subject was too personal since he seemed to be clueless in the empathy stakes.

'I have very good reasons for asking such questions,' Ari declared. 'There is a situation in my life at present which appears to bear some resemblance to *your* childhood experiences.'

'Oh...' Cleo drained her wine and set the empty glass down on the coffee table with a snap, demurring when he offered her a refill. Her brain was concentrated on striving to work out what situation in his life could possibly lead to such questions.

In the dragging silence the doorbell rang.

'That will be the food.' Ari strode off to answer it.

I'm dining with a billionaire, Cleo reminded herself, pinching a slender denim-clad thigh to reassure herself that she was not dreaming while the buzz of voices, the sound of a trolley and the chink of china and glass sounded in the background.

'Cleo!' Ari called, and he sounded just like a boss and she grinned then, her discomfiture vanquished by *that* tone.

She crossed the hall into the dining room and sank down at the table, her chair pulled out by a hovering waiter.

'If you answer my questions, I would be very grateful,' Ari informed her once the front door thudded closed again on the waiter.

Cleo had to swallow hard on her mouth-watering steak because she was unable to imagine any situation in which her input could possibly be helpful to Ari Stefanos. 'What relevance could my very ordinary life have to do with anything in yours?' she asked quietly.

Ari studied her. 'Is it possible for me to trust

you not to run to the nearest tabloid newspaper to sell a story?'

Cleo stared back at him in wonderment. 'You've had someone do that to you?'

Ari gave her a brusque nod of confirmation.

'I wouldn't sink that low!' she declared with convincing sincerity. 'I *swear* I wouldn't!'

Ari reached a decision and set down his cutlery. 'Okay. Recently I learned to my astonishment that, through my father, I have half-siblings...'

'My goodness...' Cleo almost whispered. 'So have I, although I've known about them since I was a teenager...'

Ari dealt her an amused look. 'Which in your case is not exactly a hundred years ago. Tell me about what it was like growing up without a father, which I assume is what happened?'

'Yes. Mum worked with my father and had a long affair with him. It ended when I was about three. I'm afraid I have very few memories of him. He wasn't married but he did live with another woman with whom he had already had two children. When I was fifteen she admitted that in her late thirties she decided to get pregnant before she missed out altogether on having a family of her own.'

'Then you weren't an accident...'

'No, but she *may* have told my father I was,' she

confided with a wrinkled nose. 'I didn't like to ask too many painful questions because she was a brilliant mum, apart from that period after she and my father broke up and I think she was depressed and that's why she was drinking then.'

'Probably. Did your father take any interest in you?'

'He paid maintenance but there was no visitation. He wasn't interested obviously in having a relationship with me and I can accept that—'

'But do you *really* accept it? And how does it make you feel that you were rejected?'

Cleo winced at that rather cruel question. 'Try for a little tact, boss.'

'Don't call me that when we've strayed so far from workplace boundaries.' Ari pushed away his empty plate. 'There's desserts somewhere… possibly in the kitchen—'

'Not for me. That steak filled me up.' Cleo stood up. 'I'll have coffee, though.'

Cleo set out the coffee cups on the top tray of the trolley and proceeded to pour for both of them before walking back into the sitting room. 'You asked me how I felt about my father? Rejected about sums it up. It hurt a lot when I was growing up when I saw other kids with their dads. And then years later I saw my father again with a woman and two children in the park. They seemed happy. It was only then that I truly understood my background. That woman and those kids were his *real* family, while I was only the by-product of his affair—'

Ari frowned. 'That's harsh.'

'It's reality,' Cleo contradicted quietly. 'It was healthier for me just to accept that that's how it was. I gather your half-siblings come from a similar set-up?'

Ari expelled his breath in a sharp hiss. 'A long-running secret affair, yes. I was shattered when I found out—'

'Shattered?' Cleo queried in surprise.

'I believed that my parents had had a very happy marriage—'

'Yes, but you were on the outside,' Cleo pointed out gently, reflecting that, in the realm of personal relationships, Ari seemed rather naive. 'I assume that this affair was your father's and that you only found out about it because he had…er…passed away?'

Ari released a heavy sigh as he paced. 'Yes… Do you mind me asking if you've ever contacted your half-siblings?'

Cleo twisted to look at him and frowned. 'No. Why would I do that?'

It was Ari's turn to look surprised. 'They're your flesh and blood.'

'Yes, but I've always assumed that they don't know about me and probably have no idea that their father cheated on their mother with another woman. Why would I want to upset them with that knowledge?' Cleo asked ruefully. 'Yes, I'm curious about them, but approaching them would probably hurt them by revealing stuff they don't need to know. I doubt that I would get a very positive response.'

His level ebony brows pleated. 'All the same—'

'No, Ari,' she cut in, using his name for the first time because she was so caught up in the discussion. 'Look at how *you* are feeling now. You said you were shattered when you discovered that you had siblings and that it's trashed your belief in your parents' happy marriage...'

As Cleo made those deductions, Ari angled admiring dark golden eyes over her and sank down on the hide sofa beside her. 'You really understand all this stuff... You see, I don't. The whole thing just came at me out of nowhere and I'm not sure how to handle it—'

'But you're on the *other* side of the fence from me. You are the *accepted* child. What about your half-siblings? What do you know about them?'

'I've got a private investigation team trying to trace them, but nothing that I have so far discovered is reassuring. I don't know when the affair ended or even how it ended, but my father appears to have left the woman and the children without money, which very much shocked me,' Ari imparted in a driven undertone. 'The very *least* he should have done was ensure their financial security.'

'I suppose I respect you for caring and not just thinking about yourself,' Cleo told him truthfully.

'I feel bloody guilty. I had an idyllic childhood. I have never lacked anything I wanted in life.' Ari breathed rawly, his disquiet unhidden. 'I have had every educational opportunity and advantage handed to me on a plate...while my father's other three children have had next to nothing in comparison—'

'There are *three* of them?'

'A boy and girl set of twins and a younger girl,' he proffered curtly.

Compassion filtered through Cleo. She was staggered by the amount of emotion he was revealing, because she had always assumed he was as self-contained and cool and calm as he appeared to be on the surface. The revelation that he was not at all that way humanised him and erased her awareness of their differing status while touching her heart. His spectacular golden eyes were liquid with emotion and she lifted an instinctive hand and rested it in a soothing gesture against his jawline, fingertips lightly grazing his stubbled skin.

'It's all right,' she whispered softly. 'It's not your fault. Nor is it your duty to carry the responsibility either. It was your father's choices that made it that way for his other children. I can't believe that they would blame you for his oversights.'

That this tiny young woman was actually striving to comfort him knocked Ari sideways. No female had ever approached him in that light since his mother had died several years earlier and it drew him like a fire on a winter's day, his dark eyes flaming pure glittering gold as he tipped up her chin with a flick of his fingers and brought his mouth down on hers.

It was like sticking her finger in a light socket, being hit by lightning, taking a ride on a shooting star, Cleo thought crazily as her whole body pulsed and lit up with a burst of heat and longing that blew her away. Nothing had ever tasted as good as that beautiful mouth of his, about which she had fantasised so often. Hard and yet soft, his lips caressed hers with lazy sensuality, and then, as her own parted to let him inside, the stab of his delving tongue kick-started an infinitely more primitive response. A needy ache stirred between her thighs and her nipples tightened, pushing at the lace of her bra while her heart thundered inside her chest.

'Are you okay with this?' Ari husked in her ear as her hands clung to his shoulders as if he were the only stable thing in a collapsing world.

And in a way, he was, because she knew exactly what he meant, only there was no time to think about the many, many things she knew she would normally be thinking about. She knew that any perceptible hesitation would end the opportunity. She also knew she definitely didn't want that. She didn't want to be a virgin any longer either, she conceded grudgingly. For goodness' sake, she was twenty-two years old and had held on to her innocence, her *ignorance*, whatever people might choose to describe it, for longer than most in her age group. For once, too, she didn't want to play it safe; she wanted to tear up the rule book and take a risk. After all, with every man she had ever spent time with, she had always been waiting for the magic moment when passion sparked and swept away every other concern, giving her that shot of adrenaline-driven desire that other women had described. So what if her magnetic irresistible lure was Ari Stefanos? Surely she was as capable of having a one-night stand and walking away afterwards as any other woman? After all, there was nothing surer than that *he* would be walking away...

A guy who lived in a world utterly removed from her own. *Are you okay with this?* He took it for granted that every woman was prepared to consider travelling from a mere kiss to full sex when he asked! Hiding her reluctant amusement, Cleo pressed her face into his shoulder, drinking in the divine scent of him and quivering with an awareness absolutely new to her. 'I'm fine with this,' she framed shakily.

Ari was refusing to think. That kiss had powered him up like a rocket. He hadn't ever felt *that* before with a woman and he could not overcome the temptation to explore it even though every brain cell in his head was telling him 'no'.

'Let's go upstairs,' he heard himself say in defiance of his shrewd brain.

'You had better not get me pregnant,' she warned him in a near whisper, because that was her biggest fear relating to sex. She didn't want to be a single parent as her mother had been with no other adult to rely on. 'I'm not on the pill.'

'I don't make mistakes like that,' Ari assured her while trying not to laugh at the gaucheness of that warning.

Cleo was wondering whether to mention that she was a virgin, but she decided he didn't need to know that and would hopefully not notice. She was also afraid that if she admitted that truth it might make him think better of what they were doing. He closed a bold hand over hers and headed for the stairs, and she got all breathless and incredulous about what she was doing. But this was the guy who had haunted her dreams from the first moment she laid eyes on him, and there was no way she was willing to deny herself the chance to be with him just once. She *could* handle the 'just once', she told herself squarely.

The bedroom had a wooden cathedral ceiling and a massive divan bed. Ari tugged her gently back to him and lifted her top off her so smoothly she only fully registered what he was doing as he freed her from the sleeves. Cheeks colouring as he eased round her to appreciate the fullness of her breasts in a bright scarlet bra with deep cleavage, she only forgot to be self-conscious when he kissed her again, and—*my goodness*—he could kiss. He made her head swim and her body hum like a purring engine. She didn't notice the bra dropping to the floor or the loosening of her waistband, only reconnecting with reality when her loose jeans dropped round her ankles and he lifted her out of them and brought her down on the bed instead.

'You have gorgeous breasts,' he husked.

In the act of trying to cover them like some shy

maiden, her hands dropped again and she lifted her chin, striving for a confidence that she did not have in her body. She had always thought that her boobs and her hips were too big for the rest of her, and that if by some miracle it were possible to stretch her to a much greater height, she might have had a terrific figure. As it was, she had always felt dumpy in stature and top-heavy.

He sank down on the bed beside her and curved his hands to the full firm globes, his heavily lashed dark golden eyes colliding with hers. It was as if a shower of sparks went flying through her and suddenly she was leaning forward and finding his gorgeous mouth again for herself. It had not even occurred to her that she could ever feel anything as powerful as the instincts driving her now with him. He tasted so good and the scent of him was even better, ensuring that one kiss led to another and that his hands were all over her just as hers were equally all over him. She had never felt that fierce urge to touch and explore before. But the smooth flex of muscles below his shirt, the tented evidence of his arousal beneath his trousers, held an extraordinary pull of attraction for her. He groaned beneath her touch, hunger blazing in his dark golden eyes as he gazed down at her.

'You are so incredibly sexy,' Ari husked feverishly, rearranging her to close his lips round a pouting pink nipple and tug on it until she gasped out loud.

A river of molten fire snaked through Cleo's veins as he simultaneously stroked the delicate folds between her legs. A fingertip dipped, a thumb skilfully brushed her clit and her body raced from zero to sixty in seconds as a flood of reaction gripped her. A croak of sound was torn from her lips, her back arching, a spasm of such raw response travelling through her that she was mindless in that moment, a being controlled by wild want and need.

'Never wanted anyone as much as I want you right now,' Ari growled, peeling away what remained of his clothing. He was entranced by her passion. She couldn't seem to keep her hands off him any more than he could keep his hands or his lips off her: she was more than the object of his desire; she was a partner, and for him it was an exhilarating experience.

Yet on another level of his shrewd brain Ari could not quite credit what he was doing. He did not mix business and pleasure, yet he was in bed with an employee—an absolute no-go in his rule book. But Cleo's innate allure for him, he conceded, overpowered every misgiving and smashed his control.

Cleo was way beyond the ability to speak, pulling him closer, finding his sensual mouth again for herself, hands roaming down over his long, smooth back and spreading there while she remained feverishly attuned to her awareness of the erection pressed against her thigh. For an instant there was a pause as he drew back to don protection. Her breath was feathering in her throat, her heart pounding as he came back to her and suddenly he was *there*, where she most wanted him to be, nudging against the most sensitive spot, pushing in, stretching her in the most remarkable way, somehow answering the overpowering need coursing at the very core of her.

A sting of pain made Cleo jerk and grit her teeth. For an instant she tensed and then the discomfort was gone, washed away in the tide of amazing sensation that followed. He shifted his lean hips and a wave of elation gripped her as the pleasure began to build with every driving motion of his powerful body on and in hers. A sense of wonder rose within her as her heart hammered and the piercing need that had controlled her only minutes earlier returned with a vengeance, forcing the level of excitement to a pitch she could hardly bear. Ultimately, she reached the heights, and white-hot electrifying pleasure shot through her every limb as her body seemed to splinter in a shower of physical and mental fireworks that left her falling back against the pillow in shaken wonder.

A wicked grin slashing his sensual lips, Ari sat up and feasted golden bronze eyes on her dazed face. 'We need to talk,' he declared unnervingly.

'We've got nothing to talk about!' Cleo told him in a defensive rush, clawing the duvet to her and sitting up. Had he guessed that he was her first? How would he have guessed that? There was no way on earth he could have guessed, she told herself urgently.

'Think about it,' Ari urged softly, springing out of bed and disappearing into the bathroom.

There was blood on him, and he knew, he simply *knew*, that she had been a virgin, but he could see that she was ready to deny it. And how did he fight that? Admit that her lack of sensual sophistication had been an equal betrayal? Yes, a seeming critique of her performance would really raise him in her estimation! Frustrated, because he was a male who always preferred honesty in place of other less presentable approaches, Ari switched on the shower. All he could realistically think about at that moment was how soon he could have her again…and he knew that was out of the question so soon, only that didn't stop him recollecting how absolutely amazing the encounter had been. He had never felt passion like that; he had never had sex that good…

The scent of her skin, the feel of her, her ability to stay natural and her lack of desire to impress him, all combined with her effortless sexiness, were a temptation he could not resist. As a rule, women didn't tempt Ari. He felt like sex and he had sex and it was usually that basic in that no one particular woman had special appeal for him. Yet Cleo attracted him like a magnet, and in surrendering to that attraction, he had not been sated, as was the norm for him. In fact, he was already wondering how soon he could be with her again…

Distract him, Cleo was thinking in consternation. The last thing she wanted was any kind of intimate discussion, not following on from the biggest mistake she had ever made in her life! She had to get out of the cabin and back to the hotel just as soon as she possibly could, write her ghastly error off to temptation and inexperience and never ever think about it again. In a frantic race she located her dropped clothing and hastily got dressed again.

Ari emerged from the bathroom, a towel knotted round his lean waist because he suspected that too much nudity would freak her out. He was utterly taken aback and unprepared to find her fully clothed again. Women didn't usually rush away from him. *He* did the leaving, not the other way round. Shock stilled him in his tracks.

'*So,*' Cleo stated rather abruptly. 'You never did get around to telling me what you were planning to do about these siblings you've discovered you have.'

Ari shot her an arrested appraisal, that having been the very last thing he had expected her to mention at that moment. He shook his tousled dark head slightly and regrouped. 'I'm trying to track them down with a view to getting to know them… if that's what they want.'

Cleo gave him a bright smile of approval that struck him as incredibly fake while she sidled closer to the door with the air of someone not wishing to be noticed. 'That's a lovely idea—'

Ari stepped between Cleo and the door. 'Going somewhere?'

'Yes, I want to get back to the hotel before my roommate wonders where I am,' she pointed out stiltedly.

'Staging a cover-up is unnecessary,' Ari intoned with conviction. 'This is a private matter.'

Cleo tilted her head back, because she was barefoot and he was so tall that she couldn't look him in the eye any other way. 'Well, that's one way of putting it. I'd call it a huge mistake, but fortunately, we can forget it ever happened,' she told him even more brightly, seeking and expecting his approval. 'As far as I'm already concerned… it *didn't* happen—'

His well-shaped black brows pleated. 'It *did* happen, and why should you want to run away from it? I have no regrets whatsoever—'

'It was wrong. We both got carried away—'

'I'm not a teenager and neither are you. I'm way past the age where I get carried away. We started out being inappropriate and then somehow it began feeling right and *being* right,' Ari imparted with level emphasis, revealing far more than he usually did with a woman because everything felt different and new and fresh with Cleo.

'How can something so absolutely wrong be right?' Cleo demanded fiercely, reaching past him for the door handle.

Ari rested a lean brown hand down on hers to forestall her. 'I can make it right. I can make it possible. I will find you employment somewhere else—'

It was the perfect solution, Ari reflected with satisfaction. They would no longer be working in the same place, which meant that he could cherish his rules of office conduct again. A voice in his brain queried that, even though he had already thoroughly *broken* his own rules by getting intimate with an employee. But what was done was done, he ruminated, and he already knew that he didn't want it to be only a casual hook-up. For the first time ever with a woman, he was willing to sign up for a repeat experience, and in the light of that, it would be infinitely wiser to move Cleo into another job.

'No…you don't get to do that and interfere!' Cleo gasped, stricken. 'I'm not like my mother… I won't change my life or base my decisions on what some man wants!'

'I'm not asking you to do that,' Ari incised tautly as she ignored his attempt to reason with her and yanked the bedroom door open. 'I'm only offering to remove any obstacles which you may feel prevent us from being together like this—'

Cleo stalked out onto the landing. 'You're crazy but you're also my boss. I want to forget this happened and never have it mentioned again.'

'That seems rather like overkill,' Ari commented drily. 'We're young and single. We haven't harmed anyone.'

'Thanks for dinner,' Cleo pronounced awkwardly.

'Cleo…' Ari breathed in fierce frustration as her bare feet slapped down the wooden staircase, her golden curls a messy mop that glimmered in the fading daylight, her slender spine rigid in its rejection. The solid thud of the front door closing on her heels was the only answer he received.

Cleo didn't trust herself to say another word, particularly when Ari had forcefully disagreed with every word she had said. But every inch of her rebelled against the secret sordid fling she believed he was offering her. *My goodness*. Had the sex been *that* good on his terms?

CHAPTER THREE

ARI WAS STILL recalling that exasperating conclusion with Cleo when his limousine dropped him off at his London Headquarters. He had been out of the country for five days, negotiating the purchase of an exclusive Portuguese beach resort that had unexpectedly come on the market. He hadn't been able to contact Cleo because he didn't have her phone number, and using his status to acquire that number had struck him as beneath his dignity. In any case, he was keen to believe that a few days to cool off would have put Cleo into a more reasonable frame of mind.

For that reason, Ari was taken aback to see a strange face presiding over the reception desk when he arrived on the top floor. 'What happened to Cleo?' he demanded of his PA, Mel, when his personal staff joined him in his office.

Everybody's surprise that he should even ask

that question about a junior staff member made him bite back further comment.

Mel shrugged. 'She quit and the agency replaced her the next day with profuse apologies.'

Ari knew that he had much more important matters to handle than Cleo's disappearance, but he also knew that workplace ethics would not, in this instance, stop him from discovering her address. He had an appointment with the family lawyer at lunchtime. Apparently, the private detective agency he had engaged had lodged a timely and pretty comprehensive report, although enquiries were still ongoing. Receiving information about his siblings was definitely something to look forward to, he reflected confidently.

By mid-afternoon, Ari's sense of anticipation had died in receipt of a truckload of bad news. Indeed, he had learned things about his siblings' lives that would most likely give him sleepless nights. One fact in particular had hit him very hard and he left the office mid-afternoon to seek out Cleo. He could not imagine discussing such personal stuff with any of his friends but, somehow, Cleo was in a different category in his mind. She had impressed him as practical rather than overly emotional and he liked that trait. Somewhere in the back of his brain, he was querying that immediate wish to discuss the situation with a woman he barely knew, but Ari was not accustomed to questioning his own decisions or to stifling urges that might impress some as unwise. Nor was he the sort of male who dwelt overlong on the mysteries of life and his connections to other people.

Cleo was tired. With her free hand she massaged the ache in her back, acknowledging that she had forgotten how exhausting bartending could be when it was busy. Mercifully, the rush was over, and she was thinking longingly of the end to her shift because her feet were killing her in the high heels she so rarely wore. But then she had had no choice because without the heels she wasn't tall enough to reach for certain items.

The office temp agency had been furious with her for breaking her contract, but Cleo had no doubt that she had done what she *had* to do when she resigned from Stefanos Enterprises. She was mortified by her own behaviour and it had been easier to leave than risk an even more complicated and embarrassing situation developing. And yet on another level, which she did not wish to examine, she was also grieving the reality that she would never see Ari Stefanos again, and feeling like that against all common sense just made her hate herself all the more!

After all, she had barely been a blip on Ari's

radar even to begin with. He had scarcely registered that she was female or indeed shown any sort of interest in her until events thrust them together and somehow—she didn't honestly know *how*—they had ended up in bed. She should have said no. She was well aware that she *could* have said no, because he had given her that opportunity, but she hadn't and there was no denying that. She had made the wrong choice, put *herself* out of a good job and a reference, and she could not find an excuse to hide behind.

When she glanced up and saw Ari Stefanos in front of the bar counter, she could not initially believe the evidence of her own eyes. 'How did you find me?' she croaked in horror.

'Your flatmate—'

Her eyebrows airlifted. 'You found out where I live?' she condemned resentfully, because walking away from him had been a challenge and she was proud she had managed to do it. Ari seeking her out and showing up again was way more temptation than she needed and it felt very unfair. 'That's not…er…very professional, is it?'

Pleased with that sally, Cleo turned away to draw a beer for a customer and ignored him. But then Cleo didn't need to look more than a second at Ari Stefanos to see him inside her head in all his perfection. Dark grey designer suit cut to outline every muscular angle and line of his tall, power-ful body, a white-and-grey pinstripe shirt teamed with a royal-blue tie. Ari didn't believe in dress-ing down for work and there were no casual-wear days in his offices. He was a formal guy, who laid down pretty demanding conservative rules to be followed in the workplace. Rules, however, that he had chosen to ignore in her case.

Sam, her current employer, stretched above her to retrieve a glass and murmured, 'With your friend here, you can take your break now if you like.'

Cleo turned brick red at the concept of Ari Stefanos being any kind of a friend. He was more like a nuclear submarine who had sneaked up on her, blown her sky-high and destroyed her nice quiet life. But she supposed she had to speak to him, to act normally instead of angry and resentful, be-fore he worked out that she had had a lowering sort of immature crush on him before they had become intimate. How humiliating would that be? He wasn't stupid. He would soon guess too if she kept on behaving as though he were some serious threat instead of simply a man she had once slept with. 'Thanks, Sam.'

'Ari…' she muttered, glancing up only to be ensnared by rich tawny eyes semi-veiled by black curling lashes, and her heart literally clenched in her chest. 'Why are you here?'

'When do you finish?' he pressed, his keen gaze scanning the colourful geometric top she sported, the fitted skirt exposing her shapely legs, the strappy shoes accentuating her slender ankles. Hunger punched through him with raw vigour, disconcerting him because he had believed, *genuinely* believed, that some weird combination of reactions had coalesced in him at the retreat and made him act out of character. Only now he was looking again at Cleo in the flesh, the guinea-gold curls surrounding her heart-shaped face, the big blue eyes striving to avoid his, the delicate flush of her pale skin, and his response was almost instantaneous, setting up a throb of almost painful arousal.

His lean, darkly handsome face gripped her gaze. 'I need to talk to you—'

Cleo struggled to drag her hungry eyes from him. But it was as if he were a magnet and she were made of metal. Compulsion made her gaze cling to his sinfully gorgeous face. 'We've got nothing to talk about—'

'I've had some news about my siblings, but not anything I want to share in a public place,' Ari intoned drily. 'When will you be free?'

She knew her own vulnerability as her heart-

beat quickened and a shimmer of prickling awareness sifted wickedly through her taut body. He was
still making her feel things she had never felt before, but even worse, he was making her feel them
when she was striving not to be affected. He broke
down her every defensive barrier and she didn't
know how he did it.

'Six. But—'

'I'll have you picked up,' Ari incised, and
turned on his heel.

Cleo wanted to smack him for his arrogance
even while curiosity was tugging crazily at her because she was almost as inquisitive about the un-
known relatives he had discovered as he was. She
bristled at having been taken by surprise. Would
she have acted any differently had she been prepared for his appearance? She suppressed a sigh
and tried to be honest with herself. Truth was that,
on the spot and in the flesh, she found Ari Stefanos downright irresistible.

Only a few minutes after she walked out of the bar,
a luxury car purred into the kerb. A male she recognised from the office as belonging to Ari's security team emerged from the vehicle, tugged open
the rear passenger door and called, 'Miss Brown?'

Cleo settled into the car as it pulled back into
the traffic and didn't really draw breath again until

the vehicle purred through a select city square of Georgian town houses and finally drew to a halt outside one of them. She had expected some penthouse apartment, not an actual house, she reflected in surprise as she climbed out and mounted the steps to the front door. The car departed again just as the door opened and an older woman murmured, 'Mr Stefanos is waiting for you, Miss Brown.'

Her slender spine stiff with self-consciousness, Cleo walked through an echoing tiled front hall, becoming belatedly aware that the house was a rare double-fronted town house of enormous size and grandeur. Her surroundings were like a shock wake-up call to her. This was Ari's true milieu, the rich and opulent environment of a male born with an entire silver service in his mouth, never mind a single silver spoon! What did he know about scrimping to survive in a city as expensive as London? What did he know about shopping with coupons and buying clothes in charity shops? How on earth had she ended up in bed with a male with whom she had so very little in common?

She was shown into an unexpectedly airy sunroom where tall exotic plants offered filtered shade from the sunshine. Comfortable seating overlooked a secluded rear garden that was a glorious oasis of greenery. The sound of a sliding door sent her flipping round. Ari strode in from outdoors, more casually clad than she had ever seen him in faded jeans and a forest-green sweater. Although his lean, dark features were clenched with a brooding tension she had not seen there before, he still looked younger and even sexier than normal in that get-up. The instant that bold thought raced through her head, she squashed it flat and reddened.

'Cleo…sit down,' he urged. 'Coffee?'

'No, thanks. I'm on a caffeine high by the time I leave the bar,' she confided.

'It's time we exchanged phone numbers,' Ari decreed.

Cleo breathed in deep, on the brink of refusing, and then, belatedly, she acknowledged that she wanted that link, and she dug out her phone.

The woman who had ushered her indoors reappeared with a laden tray, which she set down on the low table before withdrawing again. Cleo was relieved to see a pot of tea on offer.

'Help yourself,' Ari urged, passing her a plate. 'I thought you might be hungry…'

'Only a little,' Cleo confided, tempted by the delicious snack foods into selecting a couple and then setting down her plate to pour the tea. 'I get a pretty good lunch at midday.'

'It's none of my business, but why would you

leave a decent position in an office to do bar work?' Ari shot at her with a frown.

'If you take tips into account, I actually earn more at a busy city bar,' Cleo explained apologetically, glad to employ an excuse that glossed over her real reasons for leaving Stefanos Enterprises. 'My stepfather runs a pub. Thanks to him, I'm experienced behind the bar.'

'I think we both know that the salary is not why you chose to jack the job in,' Ari murmured softly.

Cleo stiffened. 'Let's not get into the personal stuff. What did you want to talk to me about?'

'You're the only person apart from my lawyer who knows about my father's second family. It seems wiser to keep it that way,' Ari explained heavily. 'Tragically, I received bad news on that score today.'

'Oh...' Cleo framed in dismay on his behalf. 'What did you discover?'

'That their mother died over ten years ago and that the three children went into foster care because there were no other relatives. So far, the investigation agency has only been able to trace one of them... Lucas, the elder twin and the kid brother, whom I was *so* eager to meet,' Ari breathed through clenched teeth, a muscle tightening at the corner of his unsmiling mouth, his amber gaze dark with suppressed bitterness and regret. '*Dead* at the age of twenty-two from a heroin overdose, both him and his girlfriend—'

'What hideous news to receive,' Cleo responded in a shaken whisper, leaning closer, wanting to offer comfort but not sure how to do it without crossing the imaginary line that imposed the boundaries she felt that she needed around him.

'Their bodies were found together in a squat. I feel sick with shame that something like that could have happened to my own flesh and blood!' Ari admitted in a savage undertone. 'How could my father neglect the needs of the children he had brought into the world to that extent?'

Cleo frowned at that searing condemnation. 'You take such a negative view of things,' she scolded softly. 'You don't know all the facts, do you? And unfortunately, with both your father and the woman he had the affair with dead, you may *never* know the facts. A hundred and one different things could have happened. Maybe the woman broke up with your father and refused his support… Nobody knows their own future. Maybe they lost contact and she was too proud to ask for help. It was a secret relationship as well, so there was probably nobody else able to inform your father that the children had lost their mother. Until you know for sure what happened, you must *try* not to make harsh judgements.'

'When you receive news of that nature, it is difficult *not* to judge! My siblings went into the care of the authorities. My little brother dropped out of school at fifteen and ran away from his foster home to live on the streets. He had a string of convictions for drug-dealing before becoming an addict. He was identified by his criminal records—'

Cleo reached for his hand, where his fingers were biting angrily into the arm of his seat. 'Ari... it's *not* your fault. None of this is. You didn't even know Lucas existed. But it's very sad that you never had the chance to meet him and that he seems to have lived what sounds like a pretty unhappy life—'

'I haven't even told you the *whole* story yet,' Ari admitted heavily. 'There was a baby found with my brother and his girlfriend, a baby girl on the brink of starving, whose birth hadn't even been registered. She may be their child... She may not be. DNA tests are being done to identify her and to establish whether or not she is of my blood. She's still in hospital and then destined for foster care—'

'A baby?' Cleo repeated, with frowning eyes of concern. 'It breaks my heart to think of a poor little baby suffering like that…but, all the same, it's *good* news—'

'Good?' Ari repeated rawly as a warm smile chased the shadows from her face. 'How can it be good news?'

'If she's your brother's child, she's your niece and you should have a say in what happens to her, unless there are other, closer relatives involved—'

'I have given a DNA sample and requested a meeting with the child,' Ari admitted. 'But what do I know about babies? What would I do with her even if she does prove to be my brother's kid?'

'That's for you to decide in the future. One step at a time. Don't waste energy even thinking about what hasn't happened yet,' Cleo murmured calmly.

Ari locked stunning dark eyes highlighted with flecks of gold on her and studied her from below his curling black lashes.

Cleo flushed. 'What?' she pressed uncomfortably.

'You're a remarkably soothing woman in a crisis,' Ari murmured with frank appreciation.

'My mum used to flip at the smallest thing going wrong. I learned to be quieter, more practical,' she muttered defensively. 'It's just how I react when there's trouble.'

'It helps,' Ari breathed, his rich drawl dark and deep in tone as he closed a hand round the small fingers still engaged in stroking the back of his hand. She was very touchy-feely and he wasn't used to that, because in his family they had all been of a stand-offish bent, rarely touching and certainly not embracing. There was no denying that her natural warmth and sympathy attracted him in some bizarre way.

Cleo gazed down uncertainly at the hand gripping hers. Ari tugged on it and she glanced up warily to be engulfed in smouldering dark golden eyes. 'Come here…' he murmured, soft and low and intense.

Something dangerously hot curling low in her pelvis, Cleo half stood up and hovered nearby rather than immediately accepting his invitation. 'Not a good idea,' she muttered shakily, inwardly fighting herself to keep her distance from him.

'Stay with me tonight,' Ari urged.

And that fast, she thought, where was the harm? That ship had already sailed and she no longer worked for him. It was the most freeing thought she had had in days, and the weight of her guilt, regret and insecurity fell away even faster, leaving a wonderful lightness in its place.

'Yes,' she murmured with a sudden shy smile of agreement.

With a flashing smile, Ari tumbled her down on top of him and claimed her readily parted lips with raw, breath-stealing hunger. Her fingers speared into his thick black hair and held him fast. A rush of heat surged at the heart of her and she swallowed back a moan as he groaned into her hair. 'Upstairs before I shock my housekeeper…'

'I assumed that you would be living in a modern apartment,' Cleo confided, feeling the heat rise in her face as he led her up the imposing main staircase, and she hoped like hell that nobody would see them. For goodness' sake, she wasn't a misbehaving teenager breaking rules, she told herself, irritated by that sneaking-around sensation and her adolescent lack of confidence.

'I was and then my father died. I didn't want this place lying empty and I didn't want to sell it, so I put the apartment on the market instead.' Ari thrust open a door and drew her into a very large bedroom, splendidly decorated with gleaming inlaid furniture. 'Tomorrow evening, we'll go out to dinner—'

Cleo swivelled startled eyes in his direction, taken aback by that announcement. 'No,' she told him without hesitation.

'No…to dinner?' Ari prompted in wonderment, suddenly falling still.

'No to dinner… Yes to everything else,' Cleo qualified with hot cheeks.

'Why no?' Ari pressed for further clarification even as he scooped her off her feet and settled her on the side of the bed before crouching down to loosen the ankle straps on her shoes.

'I don't want to be seen out with you!' Cleo told

him in a rush. 'This…*us*…it's a crazy fling. Let's keep it under the radar.'

His flaring black brows elevated. 'I don't think I've ever met a woman who was ashamed of me before—'

'For goodness' sake, it's not like that!' Cleo protested. 'I just don't think this is a relationship meant for public consumption. You know that you and me won't last for five minutes, so why bother? I don't want the media attention either. When I go for another office job, it wouldn't do me any favours if I've been labelled as one of your cast-offs on the internet.'

'Why am I the one feeling like a cast-off right now?' Ari enquired drily.

'Because you're so used to being marched out and shown off like a trophy by women that you now think you're being slighted,' Cleo told him squarely. 'But no insult was intended.'

Ari laughed, helplessly amused by her blunt and irreverent outlook. Cleo was new and fresh in a way that consistently grabbed his interest. And his desire for her and hers for him were off-the-charts hot. Her careless designation of their intimacy as being a fling had sharply disconcerted him, but, in truth, he was probably in agreement with that sentiment. Presumably, what they had would burn out and die as quickly as it had started, and in the short term, why should they need to complicate that? He lifted her small curvy body up to him and ravished her parted lips with his, his tongue delving deep.

Cleo shuddered in his grasp, her nipples tightening, damp infiltrating the heat building between her thighs. He came down on the bed with her, reaching behind himself to haul off the sweater he wore in a very masculine movement. Muscles flexing, he cast it aside and studied her, tawny eyes ablaze with hunger, and her tummy flipped as if she were on a big dipper.

'I wanted to eat you alive again the instant I saw you standing behind that bar, *koukla mou*,' he growled. 'I don't know what it is about you—'

'Or I you,' Cleo cut in, slender fingers stroking down over his bronzed torso and the cut lines of his muscles with a tactile delight that she could not help savouring.

Ari lifted her top over her head and embarked on her skirt. She wriggled out of it, her heart racing with wicked anticipation. As her bra fell away, he cupped her full breasts and groaned, pressing her back on the bed to explore her lush curves, lingering on the stiff little buds of her straining nipples and then lowering his mouth there. As he captured a straining peak between his lips and gently tugged, she gasped out loud and her back arched.

He lingered there, grazing her with the edges of his teeth, licking the hard buds with hungry energy before he shifted down the bed to pay attention to an even more sensitive area.

Cleo's head whipped back and forth on the pillow as her breath sobbed in her throat. Waves of increasing delight were gripping her pelvis. Her fingers were locked into his black hair, shock at what she was allowing silenced by the amount of pleasure flooding her. And then it came, the ultimate wash of sensation that lit her up like a firework display, and she cried out, her body convulsing and writhing in ecstasy. Liquid heat and relaxation surged in the moments afterwards.

'No, you're not going to sleep on me now,' Ari warned her, lifting her with strong hands and turning her over, urging her up onto her knees before reaching for the top of the nightstand to grab a foil wrapper and tear it open with his teeth.

He tugged her hips back to him and plunged boldly into her tingling damp channel in almost the same movement, and a charge of indescribable excitement roared through her as her body stretched to accommodate him. She felt possessed, dominated, and it was a huge turn-on that added to an already intense experience. His hands firm on her hips, he quickened his pace. Claiming her with fierce thrusts, he made her body hum and pulse with raw hunger and impatience for the satisfaction that only he could deliver. As the sensual tide of sensation swelled and overwhelmed her on every level, another orgasm engulfed her and she cried out his name, helpless in the hold of that thundering charge of elation.

As she slumped flat on the bed beneath him, Ari snatched in a shuddering breath and flung himself back on the bed beside her. He snaked out an arm and gathered her to him. 'That was amazing,' he muttered thickly.

'I should go home,' Cleo announced with conviction, spooked by a sudden clingy craving to turn into the shelter offered by that arm of his and embrace that closeness.

His hold tightened. 'Stay—'

'I have a shift in the morning. I need a change of clothes—'

'I'll take you home early to change,' Ari spelt out insistently.

But Cleo had already made up her mind. They were having a fling. They were not in a relationship. The way she saw it, that meant she shouldn't stay overnight. Observing those limits would keep everything tidier and ensure that she never forgot where she stood with him. She couldn't afford to get too comfortable with Ari Stefanos. She didn't want to get attached to him and then get hurt.

Sleeping over was a step too far in the wrong direction. Her warning was that dangerous desire to cuddle him! Best to keep everything casual, she reasoned ruefully, troubled by her craving to stay with him longer.

'No, I've got to go,' Cleo spelt out briskly in defiance of an instinct that she interpreted as weak. She slid out of bed, still half concealed by the sheet, and reached for her discarded clothes.

'You're not even staying for a shower?' Ari shot at her.

'I can freshen up at home,' she told him firmly.

Seated on a corner of the bed, she dressed, only as she stood registering that the silence that had spread was leaping and bouncing with hostile undertones. She turned her head and encountered brooding dark golden eyes that glittered like the heart of a fire.

'If you walk out of here now, you don't come back...*ever*,' Ari framed in a deceptively quiet voice.

Cleo froze in shock at that warning. 'I don't respond well to threats—'

'Then be reasonable, rather than offensive,' Ari advised, pulling himself up against the pillows.

He looked so beautiful lounging there against the white bedding that he stole the very breath from her lungs. Black hair wildly tousled by her clutching hands, she recalled in mortification, dark deep-set eyes fiercely intent on her below his slashing ebony brows, his bronzed muscular perfection never on more magnificent display.

A knot formed in her throat, threatening to choke her, and tension held her fast. 'You don't mean that—'

'Walk away and find out,' Ari invited in a raw undertone of challenge she had never heard from him before.

'Why are you behaving like this?' Cleo demanded in consternation. 'I haven't done anything offensive!'

'You won't be seen out in my company. You won't spend the night either? That's offensive,' Ari contradicted without hesitation.

'Are you telling me that you a-always spend the night with the women you—?' she began, stumbling over the words that she did not wish to say out loud, and even that sensitivity inflamed her. Ari Stefanos didn't belong to her. She had no right to feel remotely possessive about him.

'We're not talking about me right now. We're talking about you and your hang-ups,' Ari cut in smoothly.

Cleo bridled. 'I don't have hang-ups—'

'Maybe I should have called them *trust issues*,' Ari countered drily. 'But yes, it doesn't take a rocket scientist to see that you definitely have those.'

Outraged at her insecurities being read that accurately, Cleo thrust her feet into her shoes.

'The car will be waiting outside for you,' Ari completed quietly.

For a split second, she sat there, her every instinct at war and plunging her into conflict. She didn't want to leave him, which only persuaded her that she *should* overcome that weakness and leave at speed. In a quick movement, she rose and left the room without a backward glance because she wouldn't allow herself to look back at him. She hurried downstairs to collect her jacket from the sunroom. She was furious with him for cornering her and furious with herself for surrendering to her anxieties.

CHAPTER FOUR

ARI EMERGED FROM an erotic daydream in which Cleo was splayed across his bed like a sensual enchantress and he gritted his even white teeth at that unlikely image.

Two long weeks waiting for Cleo to apologise had sharpened his temper because intelligence was warning him that Cleo would sit him out. Even that he should guess that about a woman's reactions unnerved him because generally he didn't really get to know his lovers on a deeper basis. With women, Ari had always been more of an easy come, easy go guy. He was heading down a very unfamiliar path, he acknowledged grimly, and yet he could not overcome the visceral desire to see Cleo again. Cleo was stubborn and proud. He was equally stubborn and proud.

But wasn't it fortunate that one of them was feeling generous enough to offer a face-saving escape from their current deadlock?

Ari sent a text.

A very discreet dinner? No witnesses?

Cleo's heart jumped inside her chest as she read the text and quickly plunged her phone back into her bag. She breathed in slow and deep. Then out came the phone again.

At your house?

She wished she could inject a sarky note. Surely his own home was the only place he could hope to offer her that kind of privacy?

And the phone started actually ringing in her hand and she stood there paralysed, staring down at it, her heart rate pounding crazily before she surrendered and answered it.

'Not at my house. A restaurant, a surprise,' Ari specified, smooth as glass.

'What happened about the baby?' she almost whispered, revealing her intense curiosity with some embarrassment.

'It's complicated. I'll tell you over dinner,' Ari murmured, smiling as he recalled the way she had lit up with interest when he told her about the baby two weeks earlier. Cleo *liked* babies. He had picked up that much just from her expression at the time.

'When?' Cleo pressed, mouth running dry while she told herself that she wasn't going to agree even while she somehow knew that she had already made that decision from the moment that dark, deep drawl of his had sounded in her ear. He had made the first move, she reasoned feverishly, so she could afford to be magnanimous. Or was she just making pathetic excuses for herself? Cleo winced.

'Tomorrow evening. I'll pick you up at seven.' It would take that long to organise a venue, Ari acknowledged wryly, wondering if he had ever gone to so much effort to see a woman again and why he was doing it for her. Why was she a challenge that he could not ignore or forget? Why wasn't he simply walking away as he had done a hundred times before?

A huge smile tugging at her tense face, Cleo dug her phone back into her bag. She knew she had been guilty of an overreaction at their last encounter. Refusing to consider either a date or an overnight stay had been excessive. Panicking over an entanglement that seemed to have sneaked up on her and caught her unawares with her defences down, Cleo had wanted to run away. Unhappily, her attitude had allowed Ari to see just how hard she found it to trust a man and that was humiliating. He had also been offended and she could hardly blame him for that, considering that he had, from the start, been honest with her. He hadn't told her any lies, hadn't given her any unrealistic expectations or any excuses. He hadn't argued either when she had declared that they were having a fling that wouldn't last longer than five minutes. Clearly, his opinion was similar, she reflected tautly.

Her bar shift flew past while she mentally thumbed through her wardrobe for a suitable outfit and decided that she owned nothing smart enough. She was off the following day and she went shopping, trawling through charity shops until she found her best option, a short fringed blue dress that had a dash of style and was a little less colourful than her usual choices. Turning in front of the wardrobe mirror that evening, she watched the fringes glide silkily across her thighs with every movement, revealing glimpses of her legs, and realised that for the first time in her life she felt sexy. Ari had done that for her ego, she acknowledged ruefully. She had never felt sexy in her life until he had come along and enabled her to accept that side of her nature.

Ari wasn't in the car that picked her up and that disconcerted her. When the vehicle entered a tight network of narrow streets and she was finally ushered out into what appeared to be an alley, she surmised that Ari's surprise could be more of a splash than she had expected. As soon as she was guided through a narrow corridor past a busy kitchen area, where hatted catering staff peered out at her with intense curiosity, she appreciated that she was being brought into the restaurant through a rear entrance as though she were a celebrity desperate to escape the paparazzi. A discomfited veil of colour had swept across her face by the time she was led into the low-lit restaurant, which was unnervingly empty of other diners.

'Cleo…' Ari rose to greet her from a corner table, effortlessly elegant in a dark designer suit, cut to mould his wide shoulders and broad chest, his long, powerful legs outlined by narrow black trousers.

'Where is everyone else?' she almost whispered as a waiter whisked away the jacket she was laying down on the back of a chair and hurried to usher her into her seat.

'Tonight, it's just us. I promised discretion and here it is.' Ari moved a lean brown hand to indicate the unoccupied tables surrounding them. 'We're alone, aside of the servers.'

With that staggering admission, Ari settled back down at the table opposite her and reflected that every effort he had made to achieve such privacy had been worthwhile because Cleo looked incredible in a sapphire-blue dress that accentuated her eyes and revealed tantalising glimpses of slender thigh as she walked. He wondered why it was that no matter how often he had her he wanted more of her, as though she had some weirdly addictive flavour. But, in truth, at that moment he didn't care. He was relishing the surge of sensual anticipation gripping him, the newness of it, the very exhilaration of such an unusual feeling with a woman.

'How can we be here alone? I mean, why would the owner exclude other diners?' Cleo queried nervously as Ari ordered wine.

'I made it worthwhile for the owner to reschedule his other bookings,' Ari explained.

And sudden comprehension sent pallor climbing up her throat into her troubled face. 'You bribed him just for my benefit?' she almost whispered in horror.

Ari frowned. '"Bribed" isn't the word I would employ in these circumstances. I offered a business proposition, which the owner accepted. Nothing wrong with that,' he declared with unblemished assurance. 'The world turns every day on questions of profit and loss. I assure you that the proprietor is not making a loss…and *here you are*. Would you be here if I had not promised you this option?'

Mortification seized her. He had offered and she had accepted, and she had not spared a thought as to how he could achieve such a phenomenon for her benefit, had she? Any criticism would be unjustified and, what was more, did she want to criticise? For the first time in her life, a male had gone to considerable lengths simply to see her. Did she really want to diminish that compliment or criticise it? She glanced around the empty restaurant and finally understood that Ari wielded the kind of power with money that she could barely imagine. Ari didn't play games and he didn't offer false promises. He had met her demand for privacy, and if she shrank from the means he had chosen to utilise, that was her problem, *not* his.

'I didn't think through what I was asking properly,' Cleo conceded uneasily. 'Considering who you are, it wasn't a reasonable request. Your social life is always in the gossip columns. People are interested in your life and your companions—'

'Let's order our meal,' Ari cut into her troubled observations quietly as the waiter extended a handwritten menu. 'And let's forget about how we got here.'

Perhaps that was easy for him, but it wasn't easy for Cleo, who was ridiculously conscious of their quiet surroundings and his admirable ability to behave as though eating in an empty public dining room was normal for him. She selected her menu choices, sipped at the rich wine that arrived and tried not to stare at Ari.

Only that was a challenge she could not meet, for he was breathtakingly beautiful no matter what angle she looked at him from. The way his black luxuriant hair fell across his brow, the exotic slash of his high cheekbones, those perfectly moulded lips surrounded by a faint shadow of dark stubble, but most of all she was enthralled by his eyes, a dark and volatile mix of bronze, gold and caramel, accentuated by glorious black lashes longer than her own. She looked at him and it was his spectacular eyes that captured her every time.

'Tell me,' Ari urged quietly as he glanced up after the appetisers had been delivered. 'Why, after we were first together, were you so dismayed by my suggestion that I help you find other office employment?'

Cleo tensed and tried to savour the tiny sliver of wild mushroom on her fork. She pondered for a moment and then murmured, 'My father meddled with my mother's employment choices and it was to her detriment. I grew up with her bitterness. To protect his position in the same company, he persuaded her to resign hers. She agreed to keep him happy and because she believed they had a future together,' she advanced ruefully. 'But, of course, they didn't have a future and, unluckily for her, she never got that high up the career ladder again.'

'A sobering tale,' Ari remarked thoughtfully. 'Only we don't have a similar history and why would I wish to damage your prospects?'

'I have to be sensible and look out for me because nobody else will,' Cleo parried, refusing to get into the topic because it would be embarrassing. Nobody would take her seriously in any new job if she only got the job in the first place on Ari's personal recommendation. She would have to be stupid to think otherwise.

'I don't like feeling responsible for your resignation from my HQ,' Ari admitted bluntly.

Cleo shrugged. 'I was only a temp. It's not that big a deal, but I did the right thing when I left—'

'Only it didn't work,' Ari pointed out silkily. 'After all, here we still are…together.'

'And it's *still* against all common sense,' Cleo said roundly.

Ari lounged back in his chair and grinned, that slashing charismatic smile making her heart clench inside her chest. He looked utterly gorgeous and utterly unrepentant. 'That's a risk I'm prepared to take.'

'Will you tell me what you've found out about the baby?' Cleo pressed inquisitively as the first course arrived.

'She's only recently left hospital and she is still receiving medical attention in foster care. She's suffered a lot in her short life…but yes, she is, according to the DNA tests, my flesh and blood. Her mother was also an orphan. I am presently the only relative waiting in the wings, although her aunts are obviously still out there but it will take time to track them down,' Ari conceded. 'I have expressed an interest in meeting my niece—'

'When?' Cleo prompted with interest.

'Possibly later this week. I was hoping that you would consider accompanying me—'

Cleo was taken aback by the suggestion. *'Me?'*

'I know nothing about babies, and your presence would make me more relaxed—'

'I spent years babysitting as a teenager. That's my only experience of young children,' Cleo confessed in a rush, but she was pleased by his request. 'I would love to meet her, though. How old is she?'

'They think she's ten months old, but apparently she's very small and she has developmental delays, which makes it hard to be more accurate.'

'Does she have a name?' Cleo asked.

'Someone came up with Lucinda by contracting her parents' first names… Lucas and Cindy,' Ari proffered wryly. 'Considering that their addiction almost killed her, I'm not sure how happy an association that is to give their daughter.'

'They were still her parents, and I think that until you know all the facts, it's probably better not to make judgements,' Cleo suggested quietly. 'Particularly when you're hoping to find your other siblings, because it's possible that Lucas's sisters may have a very different outlook on what happened to their brother.'

Ari nodded. 'A fair point,' he commented with a smile. 'Making snap judgements is a habit of mine—'

'You're an only child. You've never had to bite your tongue to keep the peace. I haven't either,' Cleo remarked reflectively. 'But I saw what it was like when my mother married my stepfather, who has three adult children. Watching them interact was an education. You and I had nobody to argue with us and challenge us as kids.'

'It doesn't even occur to me to think about stuff of that nature,' Ari admitted. 'When did your mother meet and marry your stepfather?'

'When I was seventeen. He's a kind man and she's very happy with him.'

By the time they were leaving by the rear entrance, Cleo was on a high following a relaxing evening. Ari was letting her into his life, trusting her with secrets and taking her opinions on board.

Of course, she felt a little giddy and had a sense of accomplishment. When he curved an arm round her in the back of the limousine that collected them, her cheeks blazed as she voiced the awkward words that had been in the back of her mind all evening. 'I can't stay with you tonight…'

'No expectations here, *glykia mou*,' Ari responded.

'It's just…er… It's just that—'

Ari laughed. 'It's fine, Cleo. You're dealing with a fully grown adult male…but, to be frank, you're a welcome guest in any condition.'

Cleo's face was beet red and she dropped her head, knowing that she would never take the risk of having to hug a hot-water bottle to ease cramps in his radius. Long fingers tipped up her chin to meet her troubled blue eyes, and without warning, he kissed her breathless. A piercing surge of sweet heat arrowed through her quivering body, setting her alight wherever it touched. That quickly, she ached shamelessly, wanting what she couldn't have, reliving their last encounter with every sense thrumming and her body throbbing.

'I'll call you,' Ari told her as he saw her right to the door of the building where she lived.

She floated into bed that night feeling as light as a breeze and resolved not to sink into negative 'what if?' thoughts that would make her feel as though she were doing something wrong. It was an insane attraction and it wouldn't last for ever—she knew that… *Of course* she did. Maybe she would never hear from Ari again. There were no guarantees in her future, but she could live with that, couldn't she?

Ari called the following day to tell her that his meeting with his niece was scheduled for the Thursday afternoon. Cleo rearranged her shift to make herself available, agreeing to work that night instead, and Ari picked her up. He looked tense, his lean, dark features taut.

'Why are you stressing about this?' Cleo asked him quietly. 'All you need to do is smile and be gentle and unthreatening.'

Ari settled troubled dark golden eyes on her and his lips took on a wry curve. 'I'm stressing because I really don't know where I'm going with this and I'm not used to that. I like to plan ahead.'

'Stop trying to conquer the mountain before you even start climbing,' Cleo told him. 'You can't pre-plan everything. Maybe you're just curious to see your brother's child. I don't think that's a sin if that's all it is. She's a baby. You're not harming her by visiting her one time.'

'I hope not,' Ari breathed as the limousine filtered to a halt outside a bleak municipal building.

An older woman greeted them in the reception area and discussed her role as the baby's case-worker. Ari introduced Cleo as his girlfriend, which disconcerted her. His girlfriend… Was she really? Or had that merely been a convenient label to excuse her presence? They were shown into a meeting room and invited to sit down. Impervious to that suggestion, Ari paced restlessly in front of the window until another woman arrived with a baby in her arms. Ari strode eagerly forward to get a first look at his niece. Not wishing to muscle in, Cleo remained seated. Ari sat down beside her and the baby was handed to him.

Lucinda was tiny but her eyes were bright and huge in her tiny face. As Cleo finally got a proper look at the baby, she was betrayed into an exclamation. 'Ari…she's got your eyes!'

And it was true. Lucinda had eyes just like Ari, a golden mixture of browns, heavily fringed with black lashes that matched the wayward strands on her little head.

'Yes,' he said heavily. 'I've seen a photo of my brother and we looked alike. The Stefanos genes seem to be strong.'

Keen to angle his thoughts in a more positive direction and away from the premature death of his half-brother, Cleo murmured, 'She's a very pretty baby.'

'And so she should be,' the social worker chimed in. 'I believe her mother was a model and quite a looker before substance abuse destroyed her career.'

'Would you like to hold her?' Ari asked.

Cleo swallowed hard and opened her arms. The baby was a slight, warm weight curled into her arm and gazed up at her with Ari's tawny eyes. 'She's beautiful,' she whispered.

'She doesn't cry much,' the foster parent proffered. 'But she likes her bottles.'

'She probably became used to her cries not getting a response,' the social worker opined. 'She is gaining weight steadily, though, and getting stronger.'

As the little rosebud mouth opened, Cleo gently rocked the child to soothe her again. The long lashes drooped and a thready little sigh sounded. Ari reclaimed his niece with visible awkwardness and sat in silence gazing down at her. A few minutes later, he passed the child back to the foster parent and, after organising a further meeting with the social worker, they returned to the limousine.

'What do you think you will do?' Cleo asked.

'I believe that I will try to adopt her. She deserves a loving home… I only hope that I can provide that,' Ari murmured tautly. 'Do you want to join me for dinner now?'

'No, drop me off at the bar, please. I'm working tonight. I swapped shifts so that I could come with you this afternoon,' Cleo explained.

Ari sighed but, contrary to her expectations, he made no critical comment. 'I'll see you at the weekend,' he told her.

But indeed, Cleo saw him much sooner than that. Someone hammered on the door before nine the next morning. Ella had already left for her classes and Cleo clambered up with a groan, straightened her pyjamas and hurried down to answer it. The last person she was expecting to see was Ari Stefanos, who shook a newspaper in her startled face and strode in past her.

'I trusted you!' he shot at her in furious condemnation.

Cleo leant back against the door to close it and stared at him. Unlike her, he was fully dressed, all designer chic in a silver-grey fitted suit, dark grey tie and shadow striped shirt. He looked drop-dead gorgeous from the gleaming black crown of his head to the toes of his hand-stitched shoes. But his expression was murderous. He was pale below his bronzed complexion, his eyes were dark and as hard as iron, his mouth compressed and his hard jawline heavily shadowed with stubble as if he had not yet shaved.

'What did you say…about trusting me?' Cleo prompted, because she was only just beginning to wake up properly. 'And what are you doing here this early in the day?'

Ari slammed the newspaper down on the breakfast bar of the tiny galley kitchen for emphasis. 'I'm here about *this*!' he stressed with savage distaste.

He could never recall being in such a rage before, and a bitter sense of betrayal ran hot as a lava flow through his veins. His suspicions had zeroed in on Cleo first because it was so rare for him to share confidences with another individual. He had trusted her and she had let him down. Why hadn't he kept his own counsel? Why had he put his faith in a complete stranger? He had never before taken a risk like that. *Thee mou*, what quality did she have that had contrived to come between him and his wits? Had his libido persuaded him that she was a safe harbour for his secrets? The suspicion that he could be that basic, that stupid, outraged his pride.

Cleo padded closer in her bare feet and picked out the headline in the colourful tabloid newspaper that evidently had Ari breathing fire.

Billionaire baby almost dies from neglect!

Beside it they had run a large photo of Ari. Beneath ran a story about Lucinda's mother, Cindy, stating that she had been a model and an ex of Ari's before heroin became her downfall. The item described how the baby had been found starving in a squat beside the body of her mother. Ari was named as the baby's father.

'Well, they've got the story very wrong,' Cleo pointed out. 'What I don't understand is why you should think that this nonsense has anything to do with me...'

'I imagine that if I checked your bank account I'd find the proof that you were paid for that story by a journalist, who decided to put his own, more interesting twist on Lucinda's background! It's much more newsworthy if I'm cast in the role of a neglectful father!'

'I can assure you that you won't be checking my bank account any time soon,' Cleo retorted crisply. 'But I'm not responsible for this article. I haven't told anybody about Lucinda or your father's second family—'

'Perhaps you decided to keep my father's affair and the children born from it a secret as a special favour to me. I don't know,' Ari grated with distaste. 'I only know that you were the *only* person who knew about my niece and her unsavoury beginnings, and now here it is, spread across the newspapers for all to read about, and now *I'm* being accused of having abandoned her vulnerable mother and left my child to starve and suffer.'

Cleo folded her arms. 'Well, the article's nine tenths rubbish, so I don't know why you're so bothered about gossipy conjecture when you know the truth and the authorities do as well. You didn't even know Lucinda's mother, never mind have an affair with her,' she pointed out with quiet common sense. 'But while I understand that you're upset to see this kind of stuff being printed, I don't understand why you're bringing it to my doorstep when I had nothing to do with it—'

'It has to be you who leaked certain facts… There are no other possible profiteers in the picture!' Ari slammed back at her accusingly.

Cleo refused to be intimidated, although her temper was steadily climbing and had she had the physical strength she would literally have thrown him out of the apartment. Even so, she could already feel the sharp piercing sting of hurt and disappointment that he could believe her capable of breaking his trust and profiting from his family's tragic secrets. But she buried that vulnerability as fast as she could and refused to acknowledge it. 'Don't be so naive, Ari. There must be dozens of people who know enough about Lucinda to have sold this story,' she parried curtly.

'What the hell are you trying to say?'

'Well, a lot of people have been involved in Lucinda's life because of her near-death experience. Start with your lawyer and those who work for him—that's one set of people in possession of facts you would prefer to keep confidential. Then there's the private investigation agency you hired to find your siblings, who identified Lucinda as potentially being your brother's child… That's another set. What about the paramedics and the police who found Lucinda and her parents? Or the medical staff, who cared for your niece in hospital? Or even the DNA-testing facility you used to find out whether or not you and her were related? Then there's the social services staff involved in finding a home for her and her foster carers. Why don't you start counting up just how many different people already know enough about Lucinda's background to cause you grief?'

Ari stared back at her in brooding silence. Cleo looked so tiny standing there, even with her slight shoulders thrown back and her body stretched to its maximum, not very impressive height as she squared up to him. She was wearing pyjamas with horrendous zebra stripes on them, her mop of curls an explosion of gold round her face, her bright blue eyes wide and shocked. She didn't look remotely like a young woman who had been caught out in a shameful money-grabbing exercise. 'I—'

'No, don't you accuse me of anything more,' Cleo warned him in a brittle tone as she struggled to hold her composure together. 'I'm not responsible for this stupid story, and I would suggest that you concentrate your energies on finding out who *is*.'

With that advice, she lifted the newspaper, folded it and thrust it back at him before walking back to the door and yanking it open to encourage his departure. She slammed it shut behind him even as he began swinging back to say something else. In all her life she had never felt more exposed or more hurt. With a few simple sentences Ari Stefanos had trashed her every hope and belief, revealing his true opinion of her character.

She was poor, which apparently meant that she was also untrustworthy and a potential gold digger without a conscience. Tears stung her eyes. Ari had encouraged her to develop a false impression of their relationship. He had emptied a fashionable restaurant for her benefit just in an effort to see her again. But what had that been worth? He was an incredibly wealthy man, a man accustomed to doing exactly as he liked, regardless of cost. It hadn't meant that he set a high personal value on her or her character. Nor had his confidences about his father's second family meant anything more concrete. She had simply been in the right place at the right time at the retreat when he had been in the mood to talk to someone.

But she *had* made a big mistake, hadn't she? The mistake of thinking that she was somehow special in Ari's eyes.

Only now that pathetic conviction had fallen down around her ears like a collapsed house of cards, warning her that she had been vain and foolish to overestimate her importance to him. The instant someone had talked to the press about Ari's private life, she had become his prime suspect! Yet if he had thought it through, he would have realised that had she been guilty she would have made much more money from selling the *real* story, which he had shared with her. And not a story that merely twisted a tiny part of the whole to falsely depict him as a mean-spirited, neglectful father who had failed to look after his illegitimate child's well-being.

So, lesson learned the hard way as always, Cleo reflected unhappily. She was nobody and nothing in Ari's eyes, just a girl he had slept with a couple of times. Everything else had been icing on an empty cake and she had been an absolute idiot to believe that it could ever be anything more.

CHAPTER FIVE

'THESE ARE GORGEOUS!' Ella chorused in wonderment over the extravagant arrangement of tiger lilies in the vase that had been delivered with them. 'You can't put these ones in the bin as well.'

'Well, I've nobody left to give flowers to,' Cleo pointed out, having handed out the previous bouquets to neighbours and workmates. 'And I don't want to look at them here and be reminded of him.'

'I wish you'd tell me what he did that is *so* unforgivable,' Ella said and not for the first time. 'He is certainly saying sorry with style.'

'He can say it until he's blue in the face... It won't change anything,' Cleo said, her generous pink mouth suddenly tight and flat as a steel bar. Ari Stefanos had wronged her in the most unforgivable way. He should never have risked sharing his wretched family secrets in the first instance if he was so ready to suddenly flip and blame her for selling them to the press.

'If you're sure you don't want them, I'll give them to my mother when I meet her for lunch. She'll be thrilled,' her flatmate declared. 'Are you certain?'

'Completely certain,' Cleo asserted as she finished her make-up and gave her reflection a cursory glance in the mirror.

'You don't even want the vase?' Ella checked. 'It's crystal.'

'Not even the vase,' Cleo confirmed.

'He's gorgeous, Cleo,' Ella remarked abruptly, having got a look at Ari when he called at the flat to find out where Cleo worked. 'In your shoes, I think I'd cut him some slack.'

'Looks aren't everything,' Cleo parried, grabbing up her bag to leave, wondering exactly how long it was likely to take for that hollow sensation of loss that she had been nursing inside her to dissipate. Ten days had passed and that awful feeling hadn't yet faded even a little bit. 'And he's already had a second chance and he blew that as well, so I'm not about to put myself out there again.'

The bar was quiet when it opened, and she was up on a stool dusting shelves when the doors swung and she flipped her head expecting to see a customer and seeing Ari instead. Ari, devastatingly spectacular in a dark suit that fitted him like a glove, his bronzed and handsome face unusually grave. She froze and then lurched down off the stool clumsily, almost turning her ankle, wincing as she made contact with the ground again.

'How can I help you?' she asked in a frozen voice as he approached the bar.

'Have you blocked me on your phone?'

'Of course I have. Why would I want to hear from you?' Cleo asked, genuinely surprised by that question as she bent down to rub her aching ankle.

'Did you hurt yourself?' her boss, Sam, asked from the other end of the bar. 'I warned you about getting up on that stool… It's dangerous—'

'I'm fine,' Cleo insisted with hot cheeks as she limped away to put the stool back.

'Take a break,' Sam urged her across the counter. 'Give the leg a rest for a few minutes.'

'I'll have coffee with you,' Ari murmured very quietly, watching her like a hawk and marvelling at the rapidity of the changing expressions on her heart-shaped face. She had given her boss a genuine smile, but the one she had given him had been fake. That infuriated him. Yet she still looked astonishingly pretty, her halo of curls burnished by the low lighting, her eyes blue as violets against her pale porcelain skin, her sexy little mouth tight with constraint.

She had blocked his calls as if he were a nuisance caller, Ari reflected bleakly. That had *never* happened to him before with a woman. Nor had the attempt to apologise with flowers got him anywhere as he'd waited in vain for her to contact him. Of course, he had never got in deep enough with any woman to the extent that he was having arguments with her and trying to apologise, he acknowledged impatiently. He was disturbed by the suspicion that he was behaving clumsily because he had absolutely no experience of ever being in such a position. There was something to be said for sticking to one-night stands, only no one-night stand had ever had the effect on him that Cleo had. And it was Cleo and Cleo alone whom he wanted.

Ari breathed in slow and deep. Hunger slivered through him and bit deep enough to make him wince as his pants tightened across his groin. He couldn't sleep for thinking about her. She had got him obsessed. He didn't know how, he didn't know why, he only knew that she tied him up in knots and her absence took every spark of excitement and anticipation out of his life. And now that he needed a favour from her, he didn't know how the hell he could persuade her into helping him out of a tight corner.

Cleo's head flew up, angry words on her tongue until she realised that Sam was watching and that, as far as he was concerned, Ari was a customer to be served. She gave Ari a bright meaningless smile. 'No problem, sir,' she said and watched his beautiful face tense at her formality.

As she made the coffee she tried to eradicate that image of his beautiful face and wilful, wonderfully sensual mouth from her mind, but it was too big a challenge. She saw Ari and a sharp little arrow of hot, desperate craving shot through her, scrambling her brain and ensuring that she just wanted to rip his clothes off and climb him like a vine. There was nothing mature or controlled about that reaction. It was a primitive urge that she struggled to suppress every time she met his extraordinary eyes.

'I'm trying very hard to apologise,' Ari proffered when she brought the coffee to the table. 'Why won't you listen?'

'You hurt my self-respect. I can't forgive that,' Cleo advanced as she sat down opposite him, eyes very bright and level, her chin at a challenging angle. 'I thought you knew me. I trusted you. Then I find out that just because I'm a nobody without money, I was your one and *only* suspect. That tells me all I need to know about the way you think and about exactly where I stand with you.'

'It wasn't like that... I flew off the handle—'

'You have a short fuse,' Cleo condemned. 'And this isn't the first time we've been at odds. We don't match, Ari. You live in a different world—'

'I made assumptions, assumptions I had no good reason to make. I think I've tracked down where the leak came from—'

Cleo waved a dismissive hand, which set his even white teeth on edge. 'No need to explain… as long as you know it wasn't me. I wouldn't have betrayed your trust in me like that. I do have standards and you trusted me with secrets, and I haven't shared a word of them with anyone!'

'I was uneasy about the confidential matters which I had shared with you because I don't make a habit of confiding in people,' Ari bit out tautly.

'I guessed that, but I still don't understand why you're approaching me again.'

'I'm in a bind,' Ari admitted grimly. 'I may have somehow given social services the impression that you live with me and, now that I've expressed an interest in adopting Lucinda, they want to come out and interview us together in my house.'

Cleo stared back at him with parted lips of dismay. 'How on earth could you have given them the impression that we live together?'

'I think the lady simply assumed, when you came with me to see the baby the first time, that we were a couple—'

'But we're not,' Cleo cut in, sharp as a knife.

'That's not to say that we couldn't be,' Ari sliced back at her with determination. 'I will do literally

Treat Yourself with 2 Free Books!

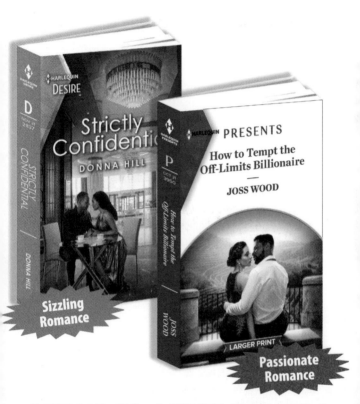

Sizzling Romance

Passionate Romance

GET UP TO 4 FREE BOOKS & 2 FREE GIFTS WORTH OVER $20

See Inside For Details

Claim Them While You Can

Get ready to relax and indulge with your **FREE BOOKS** and more!

Claim up to FOUR NEW BOOKS & TWO MYSTERY GIFTS – absolutely FREE!

Dear Reader,

We both know life can be difficult at times. That's why it's important to treat yourself so you can relax and recharge once in a while.

And I'd like to help you do this by sending you this amazing offer of up to FOUR brand new full length FREE BOOKS that WE pay for.

This is everything I have ready to send to you right now:

Try **Harlequin® Desire** books featuring the worlds of the American elite with juicy plot twists, delicious sensuality and intriguing scandal.

Try **Harlequin Presents® Larger-Print** books featuring the glamorous lives of royals and billionaires in a world of exotic locations, where passion knows no bounds.

Or **TRY BOTH!**

All we ask in return is that you answer 4 simple questions on the attached Treat Yourself survey. You'll get **Two Free Books** and **Two Mystery Gifts** from each series you try, *altogether worth over $20*! Who could pass up a deal like that?

Sincerely,

Pam Powers

Harlequin Reader Service

Treat Yourself to Free Books and Free Gifts.

Answer 4 fun questions and get rewarded.

We love to connect with our readers!
Please tell us a little about you...

	YES	NO
1. I LOVE reading a good book.	○	○
2. I indulge and "treat" myself often.	○	○
3. I love getting FREE things.	○	○
4. Reading is one of my favorite activities.	○	○

TREAT YOURSELF • Pick your 2 Free Books...

Yes! Please send me my Free Books from each series I select and Free Mystery Gifts. I understand that I am under no obligation to buy anything, as explained on the back of this card.

Which do you prefer?

❏ **Harlequin Desire®** 225/326 HDL GRAN
❏ **Harlequin Presents® Larger-Print** 176/376 HDL GRAN
❏ **Try Both** 225/326 & 176/376 HDL GRAY

FIRST NAME   LAST NAME

ADDRESS

APT.#   CITY

STATE/PROV.   ZIP/POSTAL CODE

EMAIL ❏ Please check this box if you would like to receive newsletters and promotional emails from Harlequin Enterprises ULC and its affiliates. You can unsubscribe anytime.

HD/HP-520-TY22

HARLEQUIN Reader Service —**Here's how it works:**

Accepting your 2 free books and 2 free gifts (gifts valued at approximately $10.00 retail) places you under no obligation to buy anything. You may keep the books and gifts and return the shipping statement marked "cancel." If you do not cancel, approximately one month later we'll send you more books from the series you have chosen, and bill you at our low, subscribers-only discount price. Harlequin Presents® Larger-Print books consist of 6 books each month and cost $5.80 each in the U.S. or $5.99 each in Canada, a savings of at least 11% off the cover price. Harlequin Desire® books consist of 6 books each month and cost just $4.55 in the U.S. or $5.24 each in Canada, a savings of at least 13% off the cover price. It's quite a bargain! Shipping and handling is just 50¢ per book in the U.S. and $1.25 per book in Canada. You may return any shipment at our expense and cancel at any time — or you may continue to receive monthly shipments at our low, subscribers-only discount price plus shipping and handling. *Terms and prices subject to change without notice. Prices do not include sales taxes which will be charged (if applicable) based on your state or country of residence. Canadian residents will be charged applicable taxes. Offer not valid in Quebec. Books received may not be as shown. All orders subject to approval. Credit or debit balances in a customer's account(s) may be offset by any other outstanding balance owed by or to the customer. Please allow 3 to 4 weeks for delivery. Offer available while quantities last. **Your Privacy** – Your information is being collected by Harlequin Enterprises ULC, operating as Harlequin Reader Service. For a complete summary of the information we collect, how we use this information and to whom it is disclosed, please visit our privacy notice located at https://corporate.harlequin.com/privacy-notice. From time to time we may also exchange your personal information with reputable third parties. If you wish to opt out of this sharing of your personal information, please visit www.readerservice.com/consumerschoice or call 1-800-873-8635. **Notice to California Residents** – Under California law, you have specific rights to control and access your data. For more information on these rights and how to exercise them, visit https://corporate.harlequin.com/california-privacy.

▲ If offer card is missing write to: Harlequin Reader Service, P.O. Box 1341, Buffalo, NY 14240-8531 or visit www.ReaderService.com ▲

BUSINESS REPLY MAIL
FIRST-CLASS MAIL PERMIT NO. 717 BUFFALO, NY

POSTAGE WILL BE PAID BY ADDRESSEE

HARLEQUIN READER SERVICE
PO BOX 1341
BUFFALO NY 14240-8571

NO POSTAGE
NECESSARY
IF MAILED
IN THE
UNITED STATES

anything to be considered as my niece's adoptive parent. If that means doing whatever I have to do to gain your willing participation, I *will* do it.'

Ari was thinking about the echoing emptiness of the giant house in Athens where he had grown up with his parents. He had been a lonely child, only making friends at school. There had been no family circle of relatives aside of a few remote cousins whom his parents had not encouraged to visit. He had visited Lucinda only the day before, but he had felt constrained without Cleo's soothing presence, although he had been ridiculously thrilled when he had managed to get his niece to smile at him. He had realised then that he was more ready to have a family than he had ever suspected.

Surprise engulfed Cleo because she had not appreciated that he was already prepared to make such a serious commitment to the little girl.

'Giving my niece a home means that much to me,' Ari admitted in a driven undertone. 'Her parents were unable to take care of her and do what was best for her. Until I can track down my halfsisters, there's nobody else in the world likely to be as interested in that little girl as I am. I can't let her down the way her parents did. I can't turn my back on her just because I'm single and inexperienced with children. I can rise to a challenge as well as any other man. Bringing her up as a Stefanos is the only thing I can do now for the little brother I never had the chance to meet.'

Involuntarily, Cleo was impressed. Ari had thought the situation through in depth and acknowledged the difficulties ahead, but he was still keen to give his niece the advantages that his own father had chosen not to offer the children born of his second family.

'If you move into the house, I promise not to try and take advantage of the situation,' Ari declared. 'And *you know* I want you and that it will be a battle to keep my distance...'

Cleo flushed to the roots of her hair, awareness shimmering through her in a heady swell, but she was shocked by the suggestion that she actually *move* into his house. She understood why he was asking, because if she lived under the same roof nobody in authority was likely to question the veracity of their relationship. Even so, it was a huge ask for him to make. Her nipples prickled and tightened and, as she connected with his spectacular tawny eyes, her heartbeat thundered and a bolt of sensual heat surged between her taut slender thighs. The wanting, she was painfully conscious, was *not* one-sided. Unfortunately for her, being angry with Ari didn't stifle her desire for him. It never had. He made her angry, but he still inflamed her.

'But I will do nothing to make you uncomfortable,' Ari swore, his lean, dark features taut. 'If you decide to agree to this arrangement, you will have your own bedroom, your privacy, whatever else you require. You will have no bills, nothing to worry about. I will take care of everything.'

Cleo gazed back at him in astonishment at the suggestion. Live in that fabulous house without expense or expectations being attached? For anyone in her precarious financial position it was a prize-winning proposition. It would allow her to build up some savings, something that she had always wanted to do but had never achieved, living as she did from job to job, just about managing to keep her head above water on a day-to-day basis. 'How long would I have to live there for?' she asked abruptly.

'At least a few months,' Ari replied. 'Right now, I can't be more accurate than that.'

Cleo frowned. 'That's a long time and I'd lose the accommodation I have now—'

'I'll help you find somewhere else when the time comes for you to move on,' Ari slotted in.

'I don't want to be put in a position where I'm expected to lie to anyone—'

'Let's not worry about what hasn't happened yet,' Ari urged.

'I'm only considering it for Lucy's benefit,' Cleo warned him defensively.

'Lucy?' Ari queried.

'She's too little to be called Lucinda yet,' Cleo opined in a rush, her cheeks colouring. 'At least, I think so.'

'I suppose you'll want to think about this for a while,' Ari breathed, pushing away his untouched coffee and rising to his full height.

Intimidated by his even more commanding height while she was still sitting, Cleo quickly followed suit and stood up. Her brain was a morass of conflicting urges and needs, all trying to jerk her in different directions. She blinked rapidly, thought even faster. She had to protect herself. She knew that. But she still wanted to help out for Lucy's sake. In the set-up he had outlined, she could not lose, could she? She had loved that house of his, too. That shouldn't count in the scheme of things, but she was human and she could be tempted like anyone else at the idea of her own bedroom and possibly even a bathroom and a garden as well. Those were the kind of luxuries she had never had.

'When do you finish?' Ari prompted. 'I'll pick you up and we can discuss this more.'

Holy moly, those eyes of his, Cleo thought

wildly, momentarily lost in his smouldering dark golden gaze and an intensity that revved up every nerve cell in her body and left her feeling both dizzy and confused. 'I don't need to discuss this more…but it'll be a struggle for me to keep my distance too,' she heard herself confide inanely and almost cringed for herself.

Ari muttered something in Greek as he stood staring down at her and the fluctuating colour in her triangular face. Hunger lanced through him and settled into a fierce pulse at his groin.

'B-but we're adults. We'll keep our distance because it's the sensible thing to do. I'll move in as soon as it can be arranged… I'll do it for Lucy,' Cleo informed him shakily.

'I'll make the arrangements.' With a sudden flashing smile lifting the tension from his lean, darkly handsome features, Ari strode off.

Mission accomplished, he thought fiercely. Cleo would move in. Unfortunately, he didn't feel remotely sensible in her radius, but he knew what she was trying to tell him. In such a situation he *had* to be cautious. He had a friend who had ended up with a live-in girlfriend he didn't want in the wake of a wild weekend. False expectations had been fostered by careless comments and compliments made in the heat of passion. Misunderstandings had followed. It had taken weeks for the male involved to regain his freedom and the unfortunate woman concerned had been very upset.

Ari was not that clumsy or naive. Nor was he foolish. He wouldn't make those mistakes. He thought Cleo was fantastic in bed and out of it, but nothing would persuade him to express those sentiments out loud. This time around, he would keep his hands off her and respect the boundaries. How hard could that be?

CHAPTER SIX

FIVE DAYS LATER, Cleo scanned her beautifully appointed bedroom and suppressed a sigh of appreciation. She had moved out of Ella's tiny apartment less than forty-eight hours earlier and already she felt as though she were living in a different world. A world in which meals were made for her and where nothing was too much trouble. Gracious living at its best, Cleo reflected, shaking her head in wonderment.

Her suggestion that she provide her own meals had been received with dismay by Ari's housekeeper. Mrs Thomas had insisted that she would be glad to have someone to look after because the house was often empty. Since she had agreed to move in, Cleo had only talked to Ari on the phone because he was in Paris on business.

A limo had arrived to collect her, her suitcases and her single box of mementos. Cleo had learned young not to acquire too much stuff because there had rarely been much storage in the apartments

she had shared with her mother and she had had
even less space to enjoy since she left home. Her
mother had moved frequently when she was young.
It wasn't until her mother had married her stepfather and settled in Scotland with him when Cleo
was seventeen that Cleo had felt that she too had
a permanent base.

Her phone rang and she stiffened at the name
that appeared, answering it with reluctance.

'So, how are you doing?' her stepbrother Liam
asked in a hearty tone.

He then announced that he was coming down
from Scotland to look for work in London and he
asked if he could stay with her. Wincing, Cleo
told him that she was sorry but she couldn't help.

'But you gave your mother your new address
this week and I assumed that you would have more
space now that you've moved,' Liam commented
accusingly.

'I do, but it's not my house and I couldn't invite you here to stay.' Cleo hesitated awkwardly
in the strained silence. 'I'm living with my boyfriend now, Liam—'

'I didn't even know you *had* a boyfriend!' Liam
complained angrily. 'And you certainly didn't tell
your mother that you were moving in with some
guy!'

'Well, I don't tell my mother everything,' Cleo

answered quietly. 'And I'd be grateful if you could keep that fact to yourself until I see whether or not the relationship is going to go the distance.'

Her stepbrother was annoyed and made no attempt to hide his feelings. She was tempted to tell him to mind his own business when he began questioning her about Ari and demanding to know how long she had known him. Ducking his invasive questions as best she could, she remained pleasant, reminding herself that Liam was her stepbrother and that falling out with him would cause grief for her mother.

Liam was the reason why Cleo rarely went to Scotland to see her parent. Her stepbrother had announced within hours of first meeting Cleo after he left the army that she was the woman of his dreams. Sadly, he was *not* the man of Cleo's dreams. But he currently lived with his father and her mother and worked in the pub they ran, and avoiding Liam when she visited was impossible. Unluckily for her, nobody seemed to understand why she couldn't date Liam and at least give him a chance. He was an attractive, decent enough guy, who worked hard and had no obvious bad habits, but Cleo didn't find him remotely fanciable and for that reason she had refused to go out with him. Teased and ultimately criticised for her resistance to her stepbrother's charms, Cleo had found it easier by far to avoid visiting her mother's Scottish home. Sometimes, her stepfather and mother came down to London to see her and she always visited them for Christmas and birthdays. In truth, she resented Liam for coming, however unintentionally, between her and the mother she loved.

Now, keen to avoid any further controversy, she made suggestions about where Liam could stay in London and reluctantly agreed to meet him for a meal on the weekend that he arrived. The knowledge that she would have to put up with Liam's flirtation, heavy-duty persuasion and criticisms purely to keep the family peace made her tense and anxious. Getting off to sleep was a challenge and at two in the morning she surrendered and got back out of bed to go downstairs and grab a snack from the well-stocked fridge.

Mrs Thomas lived in an apartment in the converted stables behind the house and was not disturbed by anyone getting up at night. Clad in shorty pyjamas because Ari's house was always kept at a comfortable temperature, Cleo switched on the low lights in the kitchen and dived into the refrigerator, laying out eggs and broccoli and cheese, thinking hungrily of an omelette. Locating a suitable pan, she almost dropped it when she heard a sound from the door behind her and she whirled round, clutching the frying pan like a weapon.

Ari grinned at her and lounged in the doorway. 'You could batter me to death with that,' he remarked.

Her wrist aching from the weight of the pan, she set it down on the hob. 'I didn't know you were back.'

'About an hour ago. My meetings finished early and I decided to move up my flight, even though it was late,' Ari imparted smoothly, faded jeans clinging to his lean hips, the top button undone, his impressive brown torso as bare as his feet. 'Are you cooking?'

'I was about to make an omelette. Are you hungry?'

'I wouldn't say no to something to eat,' Ari replied lightly. 'How are you finding it here?'

'How could I complain? I've never been so comfortable in my life,' she told him truthfully. 'You said that we had that interview with the authorities the day after tomorrow. Is there anything else I need to know?'

'We have another meeting with Lucy tomorrow morning. I was hoping you would want to come to that as well.'

'I wouldn't miss it,' Cleo said with an easy smile, striving not to be so conscious of his presence or of her own state of undress.

For goodness' sake, they were adults, not feckless teenagers to whom an inch of bare flesh could be an incitement. She was wearing shorts and a loose tee, not a bikini. Why, then, was she alarmingly aware of his gaze on her slender thighs? He wasn't staring. No, Ari was far too polite and controlled to betray himself like that. She chopped ingredients while stealing feverish glances at him where he sat at the island, one long leg braced on the floor, a powerful muscular thigh flexing below the worn denim that emphasised the bulge at his crotch. Her face burning scarlet, she dragged her attention from him and threw together the omelettes without further ado.

'This is good,' Ari remarked as he ate heartily, allowing himself only a brief glance in her direction because he was ridiculously aware of the curvy, highly feminine little body concealed by her pyjamas. The level of his awareness astounded him. He was accustomed to regular exposure to half-naked female bodies in clubs, on yachts, beaches and at parties. Wherever he went he met women who wore less clothing than she did, and he shouldn't be susceptible to even the smallest show of Cleo's body…but he *was*. Cleo only had to move for her full breasts to shift beneath her top, pert nipples poking out beneath the cotton, and he was as mesmerised as a teenage boy.

'It's a quick, easy option. Your housekeeper is

treating me like royalty. This is the first time I've cooked since I moved in.'

'I'm glad you're here. I have a party to attend on Saturday evening. It would seal our couple status if you appear with me in public. I'm not sure we can be very convincing without a public appearance or two.'

'No can do. I'm meeting someone for dinner on Saturday night.'

Ari stiffened, a shard of outrage flaming through him, even though he knew that he was not entitled to that reaction. 'You have a…*date*?'

'Wrong word for it, although *he'll* probably treat it like a date,' Cleo replied ruefully, her mouth tightening with resentment. 'My stepbrother is down in London and, much though I'd prefer not to, I have to be friendly to keep the family happy.'

'If he's family, he can attend the party with us,' Ari suggested.

Cleo cringed at the prospect. 'No, that wouldn't do. He might be rude to you. I told him that we were living together and he was furious. It's none of his business but he pulls the big-brother act when it suits him and reserves the right to criticise. I don't want a truckload of misinformation going back to my mother if I can avoid it.'

'If you don't like this guy, you shouldn't have to spend time with him,' Ari asserted.

'I wish it were that simple, but I'll use my living situation to put some more distance between me and Liam,' Cleo confided. 'If I talk about us like we're a proper couple, it'll put him off…hopefully.'

'Or if he's the average male, it might only make him try harder.'

'I can handle Liam,' Cleo said ruefully. 'I just wish I didn't have to and that the family would accept that I'm not interested in him.'

'Why do your family want you to be together?'

'Because he decided that he wants to be with me and the family approve. To be fair, other women find him fanciable.'

Reluctant amusement glimmered in Ari's gorgeous eyes. 'I may not come from your world, but at least you fan—'

Cleo leant across the gap between them and rested her fingers against his parted lips to silence the words she could see ready to tumble off his tongue. 'Don't you dare say that I fancy you!'

A slanting irreverent grin illuminated his darkly handsome features and he nipped at her lingering fingertip, making her jump. 'Even if it's true?'

'Don't be vain,' she urged, leaning back from him, overpowered by his masculinity that close. The scent of him was tugging at her nostrils, an intoxicating combination of musk, mint and the faintest hint of some exotic cologne. Even the smell of Ari Stefanos made her fill her lungs like an addict and left her dizzy.

'I was being frank,' Ari countered huskily.

'And don't be provocative either,' she added jerkily, stiffening in the midst of a sizzling encounter with his glittering dark golden gaze. With an effort she dropped her head only to find herself looking instead at the impressive pecs and abs delineating his chest and stomach below his sleek bronzed skin. Her mouth ran dry, hunger stirring in an almost painful surge, her breasts swelling and her nipples pinching taut while a hollow ache throbbed at the heart of her. She pressed her bottom down hard on the stool in an effort to ward off that craving.

'I wasn't trying to be provocative.' Ari breathed in slow and deep, his chest swelling. 'But I take just one look at you when I get this close and all I can think about—'

'Me too,' Cleo cut in, instinctively leaning forward to close the gap between them, on such an edge of anticipation that she could barely breathe.

'I promised not to make you feel uncomfortable here,' Ari reminded her in a frustrated undertone.

'I'm only uncomfortable because you're not touching me,' Cleo mumbled, craving his mouth so badly she ached.

'Is that an invitation?' Ari growled as he slid off the stool to stand in front of her.

In answer, Cleo succumbed to temptation and rested her palms against his warm chest, letting her hands slowly trace down over the ridged planes of his abdomen. Her heart was racing, her breath coming in short choppy waves, her body tight with an urgent tension that literally hurt to withstand.

Without further hesitation, Ari knotted long fingers into her sleep-tousled curls and crushed her soft pink lips under his. Her tongue tangled with his as a big hand curved to her hip to urge her into connection with the urgent hardness pushing against his zip. Excitement leapt and flared inside her and a hot melting sensation in her pelvis turned her body boneless.

Desire simmered and boiled through Ari. He remembered the boundaries he had sworn to observe, the caution he had planned to exercise, and he marvelled at the effect Cleo had on him. None of those reservations could stand against the charge of unfamiliar recklessness powering him. Her hands ran lightly down his body to his thighs, scorching him wherever her exploring fingers touched. She dropped to her knees and pure anticipation ran riot through him.

She unzipped his jeans, found him with her stroking fingers, tracing the powerful heat and urgency of him. He wanted more, he wanted more before she even got properly started. And she was definitely a little clumsy at what she was doing, but her sheer enthusiasm could have levelled entire cities. The fleeting graze of her teeth didn't have the slightest impact on the wild flare of excitement flaring through Ari and expanding at an exponential rate. He exulted in the satisfying suspicion that he could be the first male she had dared to appreciate in such a way.

Long brown fingers smoothed through her tumbled hair and he groaned out loud with pleasure. Cleo glowed with a sense of achievement and then he was pulling her up, lifting her up onto the granite counter behind her to peel off her pyjamas.

'Remind me to buy you some proper lingerie,' Ari husked as he spread her thighs and bent his dark head, shifting with predatory grace to utilise his carnal mouth on the tiny bundle of nerve endings screaming for his attention.

On the brink of telling him that he would not be buying her any clothing and that any he did buy would not be worn, Cleo lost her concentration. She lost it so completely that the heart-pounding, pulsing wave of bliss that seized her utterly consumed her, and for a few timeless moments in the grip of that powerful climax she honestly felt as though she had left her body.

'I need to go upstairs and get protection,' Ari breathed raggedly.

'I'm on the pill now,' Cleo told him. 'After what happened at the retreat, I decided it would be safer to protect myself, but if there's a risk that *you* may—'

'I was tested last month and I haven't been with anyone but you since.'

That information pleased Cleo enormously and she smiled at him.

Mere seconds later, Ari lifted her and sank into her hard and deep, and her spine arched and she moaned, because her swollen flesh was already so exquisitely sensitive. The pleasure was intense, and excitement roared through her afresh as Ari ensured that she did not have time to begin worrying. As another exhilarating surge of pleasure rocked her, she gave herself up to the moment, suddenly rejoicing in the freedom to do exactly as she liked.

With every lithe erotic thrust, sensation piled on sensation and she quivered at the shocking intensity of what she was feeling. Her heart was pounding, her pulses racing, and suddenly she was in a fever of excitement for the finishing line again. And she was there in the heart of the flame, fireworks flaring inside her and the colours of the rainbow in her dazed eyes as the wild fevered hunger rose to an agonising peak and then slowly brought her down to earth again.

Ari felt intoxicated by pleasure as he began to pull back from her. He had never wanted anyone as much as he wanted her, had never dreamt that he could go from day to day reliving intimate moments with one particular woman and counting the hours until he could see her again. In truth, he had flown back late the previous evening purely to ensure that he could have breakfast with Cleo. What had transpired since that modest goal inflamed him all the more.

As Ari stepped back, Cleo slid naked off the counter, shocked by her surroundings, and she stooped to grab up her pyjamas. Long fingers closed over her wrist. 'Where are you going?'

Cleo breathed in deep. 'I thought—'

'No, you're staying,' Ari incised succinctly as he bent down to lift her up into his arms, naked and flushed. 'Tonight, I don't want to feel like a one-night stand whom you can't wait to escape again.'

'I didn't mean it that way. I just thought—'

'You think the wrong things sometimes, especially around me,' Ari told her lethally. 'I want you here in the morning, so that I can have you again… although I could always grab you out of your room at a mutually agreeable hour—'

Cleo grinned. 'Seems a little complicated… but like this…er… It's totally casual, no strings… okay?'

'You're quite happy for me to be with other women?' Ari intoned in apparent surprise. 'I'm sorry, but I'm not happy to offer you the same freedom—'

'I didn't say that.'

'So, not so totally casual, after all,' Ari murmured in soft and sweet conclusion.

'Why does everything have to get so complex? Why does everything have to have a label?' Cleo lamented.

'Does it matter as long as we're both content with the status quo?' Ari dropped her down on a big bed in a low-lit bedroom.

Cleo abandoned her crumpled pyjamas and curled up into a tight ball of anxiety. She didn't want to get content with him or used to him. She didn't want to get hurt again. Ari made demands and then got annoyed when she failed to deliver. If she had more backbone, she would return to her own room.

While she considered that defiant option, Ari ran a hand down over her hip and flipped her round and back into his arms. 'Go to sleep. I can feel you stressing from here.' He sighed. 'What time do you start work? I'll drop you off after we've seen Lucy.'

An hour later, aware that Ari had fallen asleep, Cleo crept out of bed to go back downstairs and tidy up the mess they had left behind in the kitchen. Ari hadn't even switched off the lights. She stacked the plates in the dishwasher, restored the work surfaces to sanitised perfection, doused the lights and crept back upstairs. Now, at least, nobody would suspect the shenanigans that had taken place there. Her face burned at the X-rated images still locked in her memory banks. There was no need to advertise her total inability to resist Ari Stefanos.

As she slid back into bed, Ari murmured, 'Where were you?'

'Cleaning up the kitchen. You didn't even switch the lights off!' she told him in a scandalised whisper.

Ari laughed out loud and curved an arm round her. 'Why are you worrying about that?' he asked in wonderment.

Cleo marvelled at his masculine incomprehension.

The next morning, Lucy was very quiet when they arrived for the visit. Cleo got down on the floor and propped the baby up with cushions and began to roll the electronic toy she had persuaded Ari to purchase. As the coloured sections lit up and a nursery rhyme sounded, Lucy began to smile and show interest. Ari joined them, kept the flashing lights going and lifted Lucy's little hand to press the button down to change the tune playing. The baby grinned and Cleo felt her heart clench at that smile and could no longer resist those bright brown eyes in that tiny face. She lifted her up for a cuddle and told her what a wonderful little girl she was, and the way the baby reacted, it was as if she knew that she was being praised to the skies.

Ari was fascinated by the warmth of Cleo's cheerful interactions with his niece. She was so natural and confident with the child that a baby who did suffer from being rather timid and wary positively glowed in her presence, attracted by her sure handling and affection. Lucy, he registered, needed a loving mother figure like that to feel properly secure.

'My turn…' Ari gently eased Lucy into his arms and wondered how Lucy would handle being cared for by a nanny and how she would cope with his absences, practicalities he had not previously considered. His single status was not an automatic bar to adoption, but he also knew that it was not an advantage. And there was Cleo right in front of him: great with kids, fabulous in bed, absolutely not a gold digger. Could it get much better than that for him? He wanted to keep Cleo and what better way would there be?

The appointment passed unbelievably fast and another was arranged while Lucy yawned and yawned, exhausted by all the one-to-one attention and ready for another feed and a nap. Ari dropped Cleo off and she warned him that she would be working later to make up for her late start. He frowned but made no comment, and she looked at him and marvelled that Ari Stefanos was, however temporarily, hers. In jeans and a long-sleeved top in line with her suggestion that he dress more casually for his meetings with his niece, he was heading home again to put on a suit before he went into the office.

Hers, she savoured helplessly. The guy with the colour-coded wardrobe that had sent her into whoops of laughter only hours earlier. He was terrifyingly tidy and organised and…she *wasn't*. He hadn't learned yet how to be flexible, how to compromise. She had watched an expression of appalled disbelief freeze his lean, darkly handsome features when she emptied her capacious handbag to find something and he glimpsed the conglomeration of disparate articles she dragged around with her every day, everything from a mini first-aid kit to a bottle opener.

Hers? Of course, he wasn't, not in any meaning-
ful, durable sense, she acknowledged, only hers in
a weird and incredible time-out-of-time way. She
remembered him strolling out of his en suite first
thing stark naked, like some glorious Greek god
and infinitely more sexy. She had been tempted to
pinch herself to check that she wasn't dreaming,
only the ache of her still humming body the evidence that she was not. And he had dragged her
out of bed, displaying all the irritating character-
istics of an energetic early riser who put punctual-
ity on the same level as godliness. Yes, what they
had, she reflected tautly, was very, very real, but
it wasn't likely to last and it would hurt when it
ended. As long as she didn't forget that she would
be fine, she reasoned as he dropped her off at the
bar and made yet another comment about finding
her a more suitable job, which she totally ignored.

At lunchtime, Liam turned up and got chatting
to her boss. Sam had a friend in need of a temporary bar manager at a Soho pub, and before Liam
left again, he had secured an interview that afternoon. Cleo wasn't surprised because her stepbrother had considerable experience in the bar
trade. When he showed up at finishing time and
pressed her to join him for a drink, she agreed because she could see that he was dying to talk about
his interview.

Liam, convinced he had the job in the bag, was in an ebullient mood, and he was annoyed when she said she had to leave at seven.

'Ari's picking me up outside,' Cleo protested when he endeavoured to persuade her to stay longer.

As she grabbed her coat to leave, Liam trailed out after her.

'What's this guy got apart from money and a big house?' Liam demanded argumentatively.

'I'm not with Ari because of his bank balance!' Cleo told him angrily.

'I looked him up online. He's nothing but a womaniser, Cleo. He'll use you and dump you again. He's never had a serious relationship in his life!' Liam proclaimed loudly. 'He's a Greek playboy, who doesn't want to grow up like the rest of us—'

'Will you stop raising your voice?' Cleo hissed at her stepbrother, noting passing heads swivelling in their direction and wishing Liam would calm down. 'And lay off Ari. You don't know anything about him!'

'Except that he dresses like some fancy-dancy model,' Liam quipped nastily, his attention on the tall, dark male drawing level with them.

'Keep your opinion to yourself,' Ari told him curtly.

And without the smallest warning, her step-brother swung a wild punch at Ari.

Ari ducked and was coming back up to return the attempted blow when Cleo caught his arm. 'No, please… He's drunk and jealous—'

His lean bronzed face taut, Ari stepped back. 'The car's parked round the corner,' he murmured evenly while studying her swaying, pugnacious stepbrother grimly. 'As you heard, Cleo's very loyal to me. That's why we're getting engaged. I may have been labelled a playboy in the past, but Cleo has changed me for the better—'

'Engaged?' Liam repeated in thunderous disbelief.

'Engaged?' Cleo queried incredulously, twisting her head round to focus on Ari's granite-hard profile.

'So, you see, I'm not *playing* with Cleo. This is the real thing,' Ari breathed curtly, closing a taut hand over Cleo's and urging her away.

CHAPTER SEVEN

'HAVE YOU GONE CRAZY?' Cleo hissed at Ari as he led her round the corner of the crowded street and into the comfort of the limousine.

'No. Hopefully I've got him off your back now *and* without having to brawl with him in the street,' Ari parried without an ounce of regret. 'You shouldn't see him again on Saturday when he can behave like that. I don't trust him—'

'You shouldn't have told him we're engaged, and you can't tell me who I can and cannot see!' Cleo slung back at him sharply.

'He was drunk. You couldn't handle him,' Ari countered.

'He was drunk because he's landed a job and he was celebrating,' Cleo retorted. 'Believe me, that's not the norm for him. He wouldn't last long in the bar trade if it were.'

'I don't trust him with you,' Ari responded with finality. 'He lacks boundaries. Although you've never been with the guy, he's already making you very uncomfortable. It's none of his business if you choose to be with me. It's time someone *made* him back off.'

'*Not* you!' Cleo lanced back. 'That's just salting the wound. You're rich, you're good-looking, you're successful, everything most men want to be. Have some compassion.'

Ari's beautifully shaped mouth quirked and he studied her with glittering tawny eyes full of naked appreciation. '"Everything most men want to be"? *Really?*' he queried with amusement.

Cleo flushed to the roots of her hair and punched his shoulder in mock retaliation. 'You know what I mean… What the heck possessed you to tell him that we were engaged?'

Ari lifted his chin. 'It struck me as a good idea.'

'Well, it was the worst idea imaginable! Liam will tell my mother and then I'll have to come up with a whole story about how we broke up and everyone will feel sorry for me and assume you did the dumping,' she complained bitterly.

'But what if we don't break up? What if we *make* it real?' Ari murmured silkily just as the limo drew up outside the town house.

Cleo frowned and fell silent as she preceded him into the house. 'What were you trying to say in the car?' she prompted.

Ari pressed open a door into a room obviously used as an office. Lined with pale bookshelves and dominated by a desk, it had a contemporary aspect very different from the rest of the house and she suspected that Ari must already have had it redecorated. Now he leant back against the solid desk, his lean muscular body taut, sunlight behind him gleaming over his blue-black hair and bronzed skin, his spectacular eyes vibrant.

'Close the door,' he instructed.

'Ari…' she began impatiently.

'I'm asking you to marry me. No more pretending, no need for us to fake or lie about anything.'

Cleo was stunned by the concept. Her upper lip lifted as though she was about to speak and then met with her lower again as she thought better of the hasty refusal ready to tumble off her tongue. 'But you're not in love with me… Why would you ask me to marry you?' she asked stiffly, as though she were afraid that he could be pranking her for some nefarious reason of his own.

'I don't do the love thing…*or* the love thing doesn't do me,' Ari murmured calmly. 'I'm almost twenty-nine and I've never been in love. I've met women I like more than others, but I've never wanted to keep one of them. But you're different.'

'How am I different?' Cleo pressed tightly, and she felt as if her world were riding on his response.

His opinion shouldn't matter that much to her, but she was discovering that it did—indeed, that his opinion mattered very much.

Ari had grown up expecting to fall in love, but it had never happened to him. He had decided that possibly he was too grounded to focus that amount of emotion on another human being. Or perhaps it was because he had never witnessed that kind of love in his adolescence. His parents had not been demonstrative with each other, although he had read love in the looks they often exchanged. Now he was asking Cleo to marry him, and even as he did it he was shocked that he was doing it. Yet the commitment he was suggesting didn't scare him in the slightest, which he marvelled at because he had always thought that even thinking about marriage would condemn him to sleepless nights worrying that he was making a mistake. But then Cleo *was* different in his eyes from other women.

'You get on great with Lucy and she needs you. I can be a lot of things for her benefit, but I can't be a mother,' Ari intoned wryly. 'She deserves a mother after her poor start in life, and even though she's not your child, I believe you are capable of loving her. Not every woman could offer that to a little girl who is not her own. The minute I decided that I wanted to adopt Lucy, I realised that

I would have to be very careful about any woman I brought into her life.'

Cleo focused her attention on a corner of the desk to the far side of him and her eyes prickled with stinging tears. He was giving her the truth, but it was a truth that could only hurt. He was asking her to marry him for his niece's benefit. He needed a wife, whom he could trust to be kind to Lucy. And on one score he was correct. She was very capable of loving that little girl and would be eager to take up the opportunity, if only it didn't entail marrying a man who didn't love *her*.

'I'm quite sure that there are other women who would be equally caring with Lucy,' Cleo declared, striving to rise above her instincts. Instincts that cruelly told her to immediately accept Ari's proposal because she wasn't likely to get him any other way. And she was realising for the first time that she wanted Ari, like really, really, *really* wanted Ari for much more than a casual affair. When had that happened? When had feelings crept in to weaken her objectivity? Why had she kidded herself that she could stay uninvolved when every scrap of evidence had indicated the opposite?

'No doubt there are other women, but I doubt if any of them would attract me to the extent that you do. We share dynamite chemistry—'

'And you would marry me just for that?' Cleo questioned in disbelief.

'Sexual compatibility is pretty high up my list of non-negotiable necessities,' Ari acknowledged without embarrassment. 'I have no plans to play away outside my marriage like my father did. No child of mine will ever have to deal with the situation I've found myself in.'

Cleo sealed her lips on the urge to tell him that he was too rigid in his viewpoint. Had his father planned to have a second family? Or had that been something that just happened?

'And of course, eventually, I would like children of my own with you,' Ari informed her levelly. 'I'm suggesting a perfectly normal marriage—possibly one built on a more practical foundation than most, but that doesn't mean that it couldn't be a good and successful marriage.'

Silence fell while her thoughts raced like trapped animals running in circles inside her head. She wanted to say that she would think about it for a while, but she knew she would only be saying that for the sake of her pride. She had always assumed that some day she would marry and have a family. She had also assumed that the man she married would love her, but nobody got everything they wanted, she thought ruefully. With Ari, she was boxing above her weight. He was rich and gorgeous and very honest about his expectations. He wanted what she wanted and she very much wanted him *and* Lucy. She had fallen headlong in love with that little girl and needed to be involved in bringing her up. Ari could make them both happy, was already making Cleo happy, if she was honest with herself, only that happiness had felt very, very risky and short-term in nature because she had naturally assumed that what they had together would not last for long. Now Ari was offering her something permanent and secure and she was discovering right there in that moment that she wanted that chance with every breath in her body. She wanted him and she wanted Lucy and it really was that simple.

'Okay,' Cleo said shakily. 'I'll marry you.'

His exotic caramel eyes glittered gold below his lush black lashes and her heart skipped an entire beat. 'Right, let's go and get a ring—'

'Aren't you being a bit hasty? It's after closing time too!' Cleo reminded him.

Ari pulled out his phone, and a moment later, he was talking to a jeweller. Within minutes he was herding her out of the house again, pausing to speak to his housekeeper to tell her that they would return for dinner. 'Or do you want to eat out to celebrate?' he asked Cleo suddenly.

'No, no, I'll be perfectly happy to eat here,' she

assured him, feeling more than a little light-headed at the speed with which events were moving.

Two hours later, seated in a private room in the opulent jeweller's in Hatton Garden, she sipped champagne and contemplated the magnificent pear-shaped palest blue diamond on her engagement finger in fascination. Blue diamonds were rare and she loved it, simply because Ari had expressed interest in it and admired it on her finger. As he walked her back out to the limo in the fading light, he murmured, 'We'll get married in Greece and fly your family out to join us. What do you think?'

'I'm thinking about how much there is to organise beforehand,' Cleo muttered weakly, dazed by how quickly he made plans. 'Like a dress and invitations and—'

'Mel will organise all that for us,' Ari incised with satisfaction as he referred to his senior personal assistant. 'She was a wedding planner before she came to work for me and she's amazingly efficient.'

'I'd better phone Mum,' Cleo said, surprised that her head wasn't spinning with the stream of changes that was suddenly threatening to turn her world upside down.

'We'll go and see Lucy before we leave and we won't stay away long,' Ari stipulated, single-minded as always, and Cleo's romantic haze cleared a little at that point because, however unintentionally, Ari was reminding her *why* he was marrying her.

'Ari didn't really notice me until we were at the retreat, and then, after he'd hauled me out of the water, he took me back to the house he was staying at and…er, well, that's when we got to know each other,' Cleo revealed in an embarrassed rush to her mother.

'I can see why Liam didn't make the cut,' remarked Lisa Brown, a small blonde woman with her daughter's blue eyes and generous mouth. 'Ari's very, very good-looking.'

'I had a bit of a crush on him from the day I first saw him,' Cleo admitted with a sigh. 'It went from there…'

'I just want him to make you happy. At the end of the day the fancy frills don't matter,' her mother opined. 'It's only feelings that count. But my word, this place is out of this world.'

Lisa's blissful sigh of appreciation as they sat outside the luxury suite made Cleo grin. The opulent cabins of the Stefanos beach resort enjoyed the most beautiful view and they fronted a world-renowned hotel. Best of all, the twinkling turquoise sea and the smooth sandy beach lay only yards away, and both women were barefoot after a refreshing walk through the surf. With the sun beating down on them below a bright blue sky, Cleo's mother, an inveterate sun lover, was in seventh heaven.

'This is the holiday of a lifetime and I get to see you married as well,' Lisa murmured, squeezing her daughter's hand affectionately. 'And you'll be nearby for most of it, which is even more wonderful—'

'But she'll be on her *honeymoon*,' Cleo's stepfather, Davis, reminded his wife gently as he emerged from the cabin to join the two women, a greying, still trim older man in swim shorts. 'We'll go to the wedding and then work on our suntans. If Cleo gets a spare minute, I'm sure she'll try and drop in to see us before we fly home again.'

'Of course I will,' Cleo said warmly.

Ari's father had built an exclusive beach resort at the far end of the private island of Spinos and it had been Mel's idea for most of the guests to stay there. Ari had flown her family out in his private jet. With her mother and stepfather, her stepbrothers and their partners all attending, Cleo had felt much more grounded and comfortable with the arrangements. She was also relieved that Liam had opted to stay home and look after the pub to allow his father and stepmother to come to the wedding and enjoy their first proper holiday in years.

'Just one thing I wanted to ask you before we join the others,' her mother murmured in an undertone. 'How much does it bother you that your father isn't here for your big day?'

Cleo sent the older woman a look of astonishment. 'But he's never been part of my life,' she pointed out.

Lisa grimaced. 'Yes, but in recent years I've come to believe that I may have given you a false impression of him when you were a child. I was still very bitter, you know, when he ended the affair and returned to being faithful to the woman he had been living with all along,' she confided awkwardly. 'To be honest, he told me then that it would break his heart to walk away from his child and that he was deeply ashamed but that my pregnancy had made him appreciate how much he loved the family he was already with. The only reason he didn't visit you was that he couldn't face telling the woman he loved about his infidelity and he didn't want any more lies between them.'

Cleo studied her mother in shock because what she was hearing was a very different version of what she had previously been told. Her mother had not told her any lies, but Lisa had given her a much more negative image of her absent father.

'I'm sorry that I let my bitterness over his rejection colour my judgement. It's not fair for you

to have to judge your father badly for a relationship that I freely entered. I *knew* he was with her.
I *knew* he had kids. But I made the mistake of believing that because he hadn't married her, he was
not committed to them.' Lisa breathed out audibly.
'There—I've got that confession off my chest and I
can relax now and we need never discuss it again.'

Cleo nodded twice, taken aback by the information she had received and knowing that she needed
to mull it over in private. She felt sad at what she
had learned, but she also better understood her
father's choices. He had chosen to be true to the
children he had presumably planned to have rather
than the unexpected pregnancy that her mother
had presented him with. Could she really blame
him for that? That he had admitted that he was
ashamed to walk away from her gave her a much
more positive image of the man.

Two crazy weeks of high-octane wedding prep-
arations during which Mel had consulted her about
every possible bridal preference had already left
Cleo dizzy and very much aware that her bride-
groom enjoyed an extremely privileged lifestyle.
Time and time again she had had to swallow her
misgivings and embrace the art of compromise.
Just as often, she had taken Mel's advice and chosen to go with more upmarket options. Neither she
nor her family had been allowed to pay for any-

thing. Of course, they couldn't have afforded to pay for anything that would have passed muster in Ari's elite world. In a battle between her pride and her common sense, practicality had won. But Cleo had, however, picked her own wedding gown and her mother had paid for it.

And tomorrow was her big day, Cleo acknowledged in wonderment. The one downbeat note in her life was that she missed Ari. She missed him much more than she had expected to miss him. When Lisa had asked her to spend some time with her family, she had wanted that precious time with her mother but, unfortunately for her, she wanted Ari too. And with him having been in Brussels on business and their separate travelling arrangements, she had only seen him when they visited Lucy together shortly before her departure. They were hoping that on their return to the UK they would be allowed to foster Lucy until such time as it was possible to adopt her.

After an evening spent over a long dinner, Cleo's phone buzzed as she climbed into bed at midnight, and she answered it, surprised that it was Ari. *Oh, my goodness.* He wasn't getting cold feet, was he? She came out in a cold sweat of horror at the suspicion.

'I thought you were with your friends tonight,' she said tightly.

'I am, but I don't want a hangover tomorrow, so no wild partying for me. I know it's late, but I want to see you—'

'It's bad luck for us to see each other before the wedding,' she told him gently.

'You can't be that superstitious,' Ari censured.

Cleo winced. 'I am…and I want a good night's sleep.'

'Okay,' Ari conceded, although she knew him well enough to know that it wasn't okay with him, but then Ari was not accustomed to refusal.

'I want you back in my bed where you belong,' Ari admitted in a roughened undertone.

Cleo flushed and felt heat surge in her pelvis. 'Tomorrow night… My mum is enjoying having me here with her.'

She lay back on the bed, perspiration on her upper lip and a wrenched feeling tugging at her loyalties. She knew exactly what would have transpired had she met up with Ari. As her face burned, the ache between her thighs intensified. He had transformed her into a wanton hussy. And there was nothing wrong with that, she reminded herself, as long as she didn't get carried away and start advertising what a pushover she was for him. In her opinion, Ari didn't value anything that came to him too easily and she still needed to offer him an occasional hint of challenge.

Flying in that afternoon, Cleo had noticed the imposing Greek Orthodox church built on the hill above the village. It was a much larger and more elaborate building than one would have expected to find on a small Greek island. Apparently, Ari's grandfather had built the church to commemorate his wife's passing.

The following morning, as the car that had collected her mother and her from the resort drew up outside the church, Cleo breathed in deep and stepped out into the sunlight. She shook free her dress. The iridescent beaded and intricately embroidered bodice shaped her full breasts. It rejoiced in a vee neckline, bell sleeves and a layered and tiered tulle skirt, which flowed softly round her feet. Worn with a short veil, the gown had a romantic bohemian vibe, which she had fallen in love with. On her head she wore the superb sapphire-and-diamond tiara that Ari had had delivered to her the night before.

'You look like a princess today,' her mother had sighed in contentment.

A loud buzz of voices carried from inside the church. By the sound of it, the interior was packed. Ari had said most of the guests were business acquaintances and friends, with only a handful of his distant cousins sprinkled through the mix. Cleo, on the other hand, only had her stepfamily and a couple of old schoolfriends who had elected to come but who hadn't arrived until late the night before.

Now as she walked down the aisle with her mother she was insanely conscious of the number of heads turning to look at her, and her first impression was that there was an inordinate number of very beautiful women in the pews, all staring at her so intently that a veil of colour turned her pale cheeks a soft pink. And there was Ari waiting for her at the altar. He looked amazing in a formal morning suit, very tall and dark and extravagantly handsome, his spectacular eyes locked to her with unhidden appreciation.

And that was that for Cleo. Evidently, Ari liked how she looked, and a cast of thousands in the pews couldn't have daunted her from that point on. He didn't need to speak. His brilliant and attentive gaze told her everything she needed to know.

'You look like a fairy queen,' he murmured softly, his breath fanning her cheek, and a ripple of powerful awareness shimmied through her taut body. 'Or like you belong in a field of wildflowers.'

A narrow platinum band studded with diamonds eased onto her finger some minutes later and the short and sweet ceremony was done. She was Ari's wife now, for better or for worse, she reflected headily.

The reception was being staged at the hotel at the centre of the resort. Gathering her skirts, Cleo settled into the SUV that would take them there along the island's single road, which wound along the sandy shore. 'It's gorgeous here. How long has the island been in the family?'

'My great-grandfather bought it for peanuts in the days when such acquisitions were not considered desirable. Ironically, he did it to prevent tourist development. He didn't have an eye for the future or the people who live here and need employment.'

'But your father built the resort,' Cleo recalled.

'Yes. The family home used to stand where the hotel now is in the bay. After my sister died, my father demolished the house, had the resort built and built a new house at the far end of the island, but my parents only ever made fleeting visits here after that. Losing Alexia here on the island devastated them and they never got over that. My mother was heartbroken because she had always wanted a daughter. I know that they tried to have another child because my mother went into hospital with a miscarriage a couple of years later. I think she had a breakdown after that.'

'That was really tragic after they had lost your sister.' Cleo sighed with sympathy. 'The last thing your parents needed was another hard blow.'

'I know.' Ari compressed his sensual mouth.

'You've never told me how your sister drowned.' Cleo almost whispered the reminder.

Ari tensed. 'We were very close. Alexia was a tomboy, the perfect playmate for me. On the day that it happened, she dived into the pool and struck her head on the side. I tried to get her out of the water, but I'm afraid she was too heavy for me to lift.' Tiny muscles pulled his strong profile taut with the regret he couldn't hide. 'Sadly, I hadn't had lessons in life-saving either. By the time help came, it was too late… Alexia had gone—'

'So, the two of you were playing without supervision in the pool?' Cleo gathered in some surprise at the idea.

'Yes, we both swam like fish and it was assumed to be safe. But we were only six years old. My parents' guilt over that decision probably made it worse for them afterwards.'

'The trauma of that loss may also be why your father got involved with another woman in the first place,' Cleo suggested with a wince. 'Grief doesn't always pull people together. Just as often, it pushes them apart.'

Ari was frowning at that comment. 'The dates would tally with that possibility,' he conceded reluctantly. 'I haven't looked at the situation in that light before.'

'It makes sense. I doubt that your father deliberately went out to have an affair, unless that sort of behaviour was the norm for him.'

'As far as I know, it wasn't. He was a conservative man. Why are we even talking about this on our wedding day?' Ari demanded with a frown as he grasped her slender hand and squeezed it in emphasis.

'I was being nosy.'

Ari laughed, his tension vanishing, his dark golden eyes gleaming. 'You look incredible in that dress,' he told her. 'I like the fact that it's more casual. It suits you.'

In a very grand function room, they greeted their guests. Cleo saw very few recognisable faces around her, but her impression that there was a great number of beautiful women increased, particularly once she had identified four, not from personal acquaintance but by the fact they were celebrities who were often in the newspapers. Two were models, one was a soap actress and another a very rich socialite. And from the amount of snooping she had done into Ari's private life on the internet, she was also aware that at some stage he had been linked to all four women.

'You invited ex-girlfriends,' she remarked in a mild tone that could not be interpreted as censorious for she was reluctant to register an objection to that decision.

'Most remain friends and discreet about our past connection,' Ari parried without batting a magnificent curling black eyelash at her comment.

'There seem to be quite a few of them,' Cleo pointed out, very much aware of the extra degree of critical curiosity such ladies subjected her to and of their often overly familiar manner of greeting Ari. An avalanche of sultry looks, kisses and lingering touches had come his way, every woman vying with the next to claim that revealing physical bond. Their enthusiasm for touching him was a dead giveaway. Body language did reveal a great deal, Cleo conceded unhappily, far from content that Ari had chosen to invite so many of his former lovers to attend their wedding. Shouldn't *her* feelings have been taken into account? What had happened to the bride's right to enjoy a tranquil day of happiness?

'How come they're all still friends with you?' she enquired, unable to swallow back that obvious question.

'Why wouldn't they be? I never promised them anything that I didn't deliver.' Ari parried that further question with perceptible impatience at her continuing interest in the subject. 'Nothing was ever exclusive. It was casual. We'd go out, have a good time, enjoy a few intimate hours together. It was meaningless.'

Just as *she* might have been had Ari not developed a greater hunger for her after their single encounter, Cleo found herself thinking wretchedly. Troubled by his entitled attitude, she visited the cloakroom to freshen up before they took their seats. She was in a cubicle when she heard several female voices belittling the bride and she stayed put, reluctant to embrace the embarrassment of meeting the rude guests but guessing that she was undoubtedly listening to Ari's former lovers dissecting her. It was jealousy, envy, she told herself soothingly, but she could not forget that Ari was only marrying her to improve his credentials as a prospective parent for his niece, Lucy. That was a sobering slap in the face lest there was a risk of her getting too big for her boots.

'I think she's pregnant. She barely sipped the champagne and that hippy dress of hers is cut loose at the front,' a woman chimed in confidently. 'It's the oldest trick in the book, but it *would* explain why he's marrying her.'

A door opened and then another, and the voices faded away. Cheeks flushed with temper and mortification, Cleo emerged from her hiding place, annoyed that she had remained concealed but all too conscious that Ari would not have thanked her for

confronting friends of his about their nasty outlook and cruel comments.

It didn't help her mood to return to the reception and find a lithe brunette in a daringly styled
cerise-pink dress flirting like crazy with Ari. The
bright smile already fixed to her generous mouth
stiffened a little more at the sight.

As the brunette grudgingly gave way to her for
them to take their seats at the top table, Cleo murmured, 'Before you met me, you lived like a sultan
with a harem, didn't you?'

Straight ebony brows lowering over his spectacular tawny eyes, Ari shot her an incredulous
glance. 'What are you trying to say?'

'All those women vying for your attention, nobody daring to complain lest you lose interest,
nobody demanding fidelity or anything else that
might curtail your freedom,' Cleo clarified with
acid sweetness. 'Marriage promises to be a big
boring shock for you. How on earth are you planning to manage without your harem?'

Ari gazed back at her in disbelief. It had never
once crossed his mind to see his sex life in such a
light. He reckoned he could see some point in her
censure. He had virtually picked women out of a
wide selection of willing contenders, but what was
that to do with Cleo now? At the point when he
had been admiring Cleo's wondrous lack of van-

ity, competitiveness and drama in comparison to other women he had known, she chose to blind-side him with an attack he hadn't foreseen, and he was very much taken aback.

CHAPTER EIGHT

'So what if it *was* like that?' Ari countered with a lethal cutting edge to his dark, deep drawl and a careless shrug of dismissal, as though his bride's opinion of his past mattered not in the smallest way. 'How I conducted my sex life prior to our marriage is, thankfully, not your problem.'

Cleo went white at his derisive tone, but she tilted her chin up in challenge. 'You made it my problem when you chose to invite every darned one of them to the wedding,' she retorted in a terse undertone.

Silence fell then and Cleo busied herself chatting to the elderly cousin who had been chosen, as Ari's most senior surviving relative, to sit by her side. Ari's best man made a very amusing speech, but that was the only speech, as her mother had had no desire to speak up amongst strangers and Cleo hadn't had any bridesmaids. As the bridal couple stepped onto the dance floor to open the dancing, the silence between them thundered, but she could see that as long as they both spoke to other people and smiled readily, nobody was the slightest bit suspicious that the bride and groom might already have fallen out.

Beneath the show, however, she could feel Ari's tension in the tautness of his lean, powerful body against hers and in the tightness at the corners of his sculpted lips. He held her lightly and did not pull her close, and as soon as the dance was over, he went off to socialise and Cleo joined her family. It was a ridiculously *civilised* row, she conceded ruefully.

The sunshine was fading softly into dusk when Ari suggested they leave. A full-scale party was taking place by then. Her family had gone down to the beach, where a barbecue was burning, a bar was operating and Caribbean music was playing.

'I should get changed,' Cleo said awkwardly.

'I'm afraid you can't yet. All your luggage has already been transferred to the house,' Ari informed her, long fingers brushing her spine as he urged her in the direction of the exit.

Cleo had taken her leave of her mother when the whole group chose the informality of the beach party. Another SUV awaited them outside the hotel with the rear passenger door wide for their entry.

Ari strode round the bonnet and climbed into the front passenger seat.

Clearly, she wasn't exactly flavour of the month, Cleo acknowledged, but, rather than her feeling rebuked and put in her place, Cleo's annoyance was growing. How dared he behave as though what she had said was unreasonable? Prior to meeting her, Ari had behaved exactly like a sultan with a harem, cherry-picking whichever willing beauty he chose from a wide pool of choice as and when he wanted without any need to offer anything more than a fun few hours. He had no experience with ordinary relationships. He was unable to see why she should feel angry and hurt by the presence of his previous lovers at what should have been *her* special day. So, she would have to show him in terms that he could understand.

After a drive along the sea road, the SUV cut down a lane surrounded first by dense oak woods and then by orchards. She saw orange and lemon trees and other fruit trees she couldn't identify before the car moved back into the fading sunlight to approach a very large and long stone- and wood-built house overlooking a secluded bay. It was a beach house, she reckoned, going by the many open patio doors and the wide surrounding terraces, but it was a Stefanos property and therefore it was a beach house on steroids.

They walked into the house, where Ari shared a brisk exchange in Greek with the older woman awaiting them. He introduced her as Delphine, who then took her leave.

'There's a cold meal and snacks prepared for us, but she's happy to come back and cook us a hot meal if we want,' Ari told her smoothly.

'Cold will be fine,' Cleo responded, strolling into an airy reception room with a glorious view of the sea and the surrounding hills. 'I wasn't expecting something so contemporary.'

'I had it renovated a couple of years ago,' Ari retorted. 'My father rarely came here, and he signed the island over to me on my twenty-fifth birthday.'

'We need to talk about our difference of opinion,' Cleo told him quietly.

'No, we don't. Let it go,' Ari countered curtly.

'That's not how I operate,' Cleo said apologetically. 'I want you just to picture another scenario. Imagine if I had invited all *my* past lovers to attend our wedding—'

Ari actually rolled his eyes. 'Let's be real. You haven't *had* any other lovers,' he pointed out very drily.

Cleo's blue eyes blazed like sapphire bolts. 'That's not relevant,' she sliced back at him with hot cheeks. 'You can still use your imagination to picture how you would have felt had I paraded my past lovers in front of *you*.'

'I did not parade—'

'You did,' Cleo cut in. 'You invited a lot of women, who were not well-wishers and who spent our entire wedding loudly speculating about why on earth you had married someone as ordinary as me. I found it offensive. You didn't think about my feelings and you should've done.'

'I—'

'No, don't you say that it wouldn't have bothered you if I'd trailed a load of exes in front of you,' Cleo protested. 'You didn't like me spending time with Liam, even though you knew I'd no interest in him.'

'I'm possessive…about you,' Ari added jerkily, because it wasn't the norm for him and he didn't like admitting it. He didn't get attached to women, although he had to confess to having somehow become somewhat attached to Cleo, he allowed grudgingly. When it came to emotions, having grown up in a family where emotion was not freely expressed or shown, Ari had learned to conceal his feelings. That had become his default setting in every situation, he recognised belatedly.

Cleo curved a small hand over his arm. 'I'm possessive too…'

Ari breathed in deep and looked out to sea as

the sun sank in a blaze of glorious colour. Peach, gold and scarlet rays radiated out into the darkening sky. Slowly the fierce knot of tension inside him eased. He got her point. He remembered how flirtatious some of those women had been, the inviting glances and touches, the hints that they would still be available were he to get bored, and he was suddenly amazed at how thoughtless he had been. Cleo, he recognised then, operated on an entirely different mental wavelength from him.

'I assumed it wouldn't matter to you because you were my wife, which gives you an unassailable role in my life that no other woman has ever come close to achieving,' he admitted. 'But perhaps that was arrogant…and I was careless and unkind.'

'Or perhaps I lack sufficient confidence to see myself in that lofty light,' Cleo allowed thoughtfully. 'But you do need to consider your attitudes before Lucy grows up.'

'Lecture over yet?' His mouth quirking, Ari gazed down at her, his extraordinary tawny eyes gleaming pure mesmeric gold in the light of the sunset over the bay. 'You're already trying to change me.'

'Polish up the rough edges a bit,' Cleo contradicted softly. '*Not* change you. You're not used to considering other people's feelings. It's not that you're rude. You're—'

'I get it,' Ari interposed before she could expand more on the topic. 'Now can we eat something? That crack about sultans and harems killed my appetite earlier.'

'Show me the kitchen,' Cleo told him with a relieved grin that lit up her delicate face like sunshine.

For a split second, Ari wanted to grab her, flatten her to the nearest horizontal surface or plaster her up against a wall and sink into the warm, wet heat of her curvy, sexy little body, but that kind of impetuosity could be deemed inconsiderate, he calculated, and he desisted from that libidinous urge with the greatest difficulty.

'I have quite a hot temper,' he muttered between bites of the snacks she piled in front of him. 'But I didn't want to argue with you on our wedding day or say anything that might upset you more.'

'So instead you simmered like a cauldron of oil on a fire and went silent on me. Good to know,' Cleo teased.

Ari snaked out a long arm and drew her between his spread thighs. 'Mrs Stefanos, you are sassy.'

Her blue eyes danced. 'You're only just noticing?'

He leant forward and claimed her parted lips with unashamed hunger. 'Last night, I would've killed to have you here with me.' He breathed that frank admission rawly.

'Last night,' Cleo whispered, drinking in the warm, wonderfully familiar scent of him like an addict as her hands wound round his neck, 'I said no when I really wanted to say yes…'

With a growl of response, Ari vaulted upright and grabbed her hand to lead her into the hall. 'Time to give you a tour of the upstairs.'

A wicked little spark of anticipation curled low in her pelvis.

He walked her up into a huge bedroom with patio doors opening out onto a balcony. The room was decorated in pale aqua colours, providing a fitting frame for the glorious panoramic view of the starry night sky above the dark shadowy ocean below while the white sandy beach glowed even in moonlight.

'Help me with the hooks,' she urged him, shifting her slight shoulders.

Ari undid the dress and she shifted her arms and let it drop to the rug beneath her. Hearing the catch in his breath, she smiled and turned round, refusing to allow herself to be self-conscious in a lingerie set she had chosen to wear.

Ari took a step back to fully appreciate the short peacock-blue corset cupping her plump breasts, the silk panties lovingly moulding the rounded swell of her derrière and the suspenders adorning her slender thighs.

'You were worth waiting for…the perfect wedding present to unwrap,' Ari husked. 'No sultan could greet his harem favourite with greater appreciation than I at this moment, *glykia mou.*'

Cleo sent him a speaking glance, amused and not at all surprised at the way he was throwing her crack back in her teeth like a challenge. He cast off his jacket, jerked loose his cravat and began unbuttoning his dress shirt, a sliver of bronzed muscular torso catching her eye as he shifted his lean hips to kick off his shoes. His exotic eyes connected with hers and he grinned. 'I love the way you watch me.'

Cleo went red as fire. 'I can hardly avoid watching you when you're right in front of me…'

'You watch me the way I watch you. With desire,' Ari contradicted, dropping down to his knees in front of her. 'I like it.'

He made that confession as he gently tugged her panties down her slender legs and her breath caught in her throat as she stood there, willing herself not to go into embarrassed retreat. There was nothing to hide, she reminded herself irritably, when he was already familiar with her body and all its flaws. He had none of her innate inhibitions.

'I'd take off your shoes, but that would make you too short for me to appreciate like this,' Ari muttered intently.

'It's all right,' she said in a voice that sounded as though her vocal cords were being squeezed, even though her fancy bridal shoes were torturing her toes, because when Ari smiled up at her, she was as much *his* as if he had branded her. She was discovering that she really liked being needed and wanted. His hunger for her made her feel empowered, *necessary*.

He ran his hands lightly up and down her thighs, gently spreading them, and she quivered. His lips grazed her heated core and she jerked, suddenly the party most wanting, most needing, and as he ran his tongue through that honeyed heat, she moaned his name. A jolt of feverish pleasure gripped her as he flicked her sensitive bud. Her hips bucked as he continued his sensual assault. Her legs trembled as the flaming heat at the juncture of her thighs roared higher. Her hands lifted in a silent seeking gesture of unbearable arousal and then her body detonated in an explosion of wild, seething delight.

Catching her up in his arms while she was still quivering, Ari spread her on the bed, flipping off the shoes and the stockings, unzipping the corset and then bending over her to capture a straining bullet-hard nipple in his mouth. She gasped out loud, liquid and boneless. He paused only to strip off what remained of his clothes, leaving them lying where they fell with uncharacteristic untidiness.

He came down to her hungry and urgent, tipping her legs over his shoulders, rising above her to penetrate her with one fluid stroke. She cried out in response to that sudden fullness, hips writhing as heavenly longed-for sensation shimmied through her pelvis, bringing a wash of heated excitement in its wake. He tilted her back even further, thrusting deep and sending her pleasure to an unholy height. Her body surged with the sheer thrill of it, and in the passionate minutes that followed, she finally plunged over the edge into another climax.

'I'm never going to move again,' she mumbled weakly as he hauled her with him under the sheet.

Ari leant over her and dropped a careless kiss on her cheekbone, tawny eyes smouldering over her with immense masculine satisfaction. 'You're my personal kryptonite.'

'Not feeling too much like a superhero right now…but my goodness, I'm starving,' she confided.

Stark naked, Ari sprang out of bed within seconds of that announcement. 'I'll go and fill a tray.'

'You're in a helpful mood,' she remarked in surprise.

'Maybe I don't want you flagging in energy this early in the evening,' Ari contended.

Sitting up, Cleo swallowed a yawn. 'Weddings are incredibly exhausting,' she warned him.

'I'm as hungry for you as you are for food,' Ari explained almost apologetically.

He knew she was tired. She was pale and her eyes were shadowed. But he had told her the truth. He had a hunger for her that seemed to have no limits and it had made him a little uneasy before he married her. Now, however, that he had acquired Cleo on a permanent basis, that amazing hunger for her no longer bothered him in the same way. There was nothing dangerous or worrying about lusting after his wife. In fact, he now thought it was healthy.

That comment of hers about harems had hit him harder than she could even appreciate. His sex life *had* been highly organised, he acknowledged grimly. He had been careful not to spend too much time with any one woman, not to favour one over another, and for years that cool, logical approach had paid dividends by keeping his life smooth and free of strife. Of course, there was always the occasional hiccup in even the smoothest, slickest schedule, he reflected wryly, recalling Galina, the gorgeous but slightly unhinged Russian supermodel, who had revealed stalking tendencies after only one dinner date.

He had backed off fast, blocked the woman's repeated phone calls and ignored her appearances in his favourite haunts. To the best of his ability, he had protected himself from that kind of nuisance. And now he was married, and he felt remarkably content with the bargain he had struck with Cleo, but possibly rather more aware now that his niece, Lucy, would not be the only party to benefit from their official status as a couple. A wife who attracted him as much as Cleo did was a find, a huge and wonderful *find*…

Thinking that he was now a married man still shook him. In a matter of weeks his life had changed course to an extraordinary degree. Lucy had come along, of course, a totally unexpected but decidedly cute development in his world, but before her had come *Cleo*. Ari struggled to choose food and concentrate at the same time as he thought about Cleo.

Two weeks later, the afternoon before their return to London, Cleo stretched in the warmth of the shade. She was reclining on a shaded and padded lounger in more comfort than she had ever known, and she had a wonderful view of the beach in front of her.

After the first couple of days of their honeymoon on Spinos, Cleo and Ari had reached an agreement that covered their radically different approaches to what constituted a break. Ari always had to be *doing* something, while Cleo liked to sunbathe with a good thriller or go for a not-too-strenuous stroll. It had had to work after Ari had dragged her huffing and puffing in the heat to see the remains of the Greek shrine at the top of the island's only hill. She had been on the brink of expiring on the peak of that hill, while Ari had barely broken a sweat. Now, one day they went out and did *physical stuff*—as she termed it—and the next she got to be lazier, aside of the daily swimming lessons he insisted on, and that combination worked. She had finally learned how to swim and she was hugely proud of herself for conquering her former fear of deep water.

Today, Ari was out diving in the bay.

'Isn't that dangerous?' she had said to him anxiously.

And he had laughed, but he had also liked that she was worried about him. He had confessed that it felt like a very long time since anyone had worried about him, and with prudent probing, she had gained a view of his childhood that she didn't like and which he would probably dispute out of loyalty to his mother and father.

There was no doubt that his sister's death had ripped the heart out of Ari's family. Instead of cherishing the child who had survived, however, his parents had retired to separate corners to grieve for the child they had lost. Ari had been left very much to his own devices after he lost his twin, yet his involvement in that tragedy had damaged him as well. Even so, his parents had spent little subsequent time with their son and had sent him off to boarding school at eight years old. That detachment and distance had influenced Ari, making him too much of a loner who lacked understanding of normal relationships either in or outside the family circle.

On her family's last night on the island, they had enjoyed a dinner together at the resort. Ari had emerged shell-shocked from the chattering closeness of her mother and stepfamily, with everybody talking at once and the children alternately playing and then squabbling. The relaxed and yet warm informality he had witnessed had surprised Ari, but, ultimately, charmed him.

Only the day before, she and Ari had flown to Corfu for a day of sightseeing that had ended with dinner on the beach and a late night at a fancy club. Cleo fingered the diamond platinum pendant Ari had casually handed her over the meal, touched the diamonds in her ears, glanced at the delicate watch on her wrist and smiled, dazed by the heat and a growing sense of security. Ari liked giving her stuff. He liked giving her stuff so much that it got embarrassing. She knew he would go out of his way to spoil Lucy as well.

Lucy. Briefly, her smile dipped. She missed that baby so much, and occasional bulletins from her caseworker didn't replace actual bodily contact. Ari's lawyer was working on their fostering application but had warned them to be patient because the authorities dealt slowly with such matters. She watched as a motorboat came to shore and Ari vaulted out into the shallow water. Clad only in swim shorts, he was stunning, tall, bronzed and muscular as he strode up onto the beach, dripping wet and gorgeous.

You watch me the way I watch you.

He had nailed that observation to perfection.

But then, Cleo conceded ruefully, she had watched Ari from the very first day she saw him. The attraction for her had been instant, visceral, while with Ari she had proved to be more of an acquired taste. Fortunately for her, he *had* acquired that taste, but she didn't kid herself that that was anything deeper than sexual chemistry. Yet, in comparison, she had become very conscious that she was in love with the man she had married. Indeed, she had probably taken the first crucial steps along that path that first evening together, when he had chosen to confide in her about his father's second family. Now he was her obsession, she allowed, her mouth running dry and a zing of excitement curling between her thighs as he strode up the beach path with her firmly in his sights and a wolfish smile curving his sensual mouth.

'Were you waiting for me?' Ari intoned huskily.

'Don't you just wish?' Cleo mocked, insanely conscious of his gaze welded to her lips and straying down to the full breasts moulded by the rather brief bikini she wore. 'No, I was just reading and lazing—

'You're wet!' she shrieked as he grabbed her.

'You should've lied and said you were waiting for me this *once*!' Ari complained. 'You're bad for my ego.'

'You don't need any more compliments,' Cleo told him, running a small hand down over his washboard-flat abdomen and feeling him shiver in response, noting the thrust of the erection the shorts couldn't hide. 'Can we be seen from here?'

'No,' Ari confirmed, coming down over her with hungry sexual intent etched in every angle of his lean, darkly handsome features and his strong, muscular body. 'I wouldn't risk any other man seeing you naked, *kardoula mou*.'

Some minutes later, they were both naked and intent on each other. Cleo went up in sensual flames as he surged into her and sated the fierce craving he had lit inside her. In the aftermath, she lay limp in his arms, blissfully at peace and not a single shadow in her world, barring the absence of Lucy. She was incredibly happy, happier, she acknowledged, than she had ever known she even could be.

Ari ran a hand down over her spine, pure satisfaction engulfing him. He found the strangest sort of peace when he was with Cleo, rather as if she were the missing puzzle piece that made him whole or, at the very least, he adjusted, somehow *more* than he had been without her. She made him see the world and the people who surrounded him in a different light. She *wasn't* changing him, though.

'Tell me about your ex, Dominic,' Ari murmured, startling Cleo, who had not expected that question. 'You mentioned him in passing but never told me why you broke up.'

With a recollective wince of her generous mouth, Cleo explained about Dominic's girlfriend and child showing up at her door.

'What did he say when you confronted him?' Ari prompted with interest.

'I didn't confront him. I just cut all contact with him, and I was moving on to work at another office, so I didn't run into him again,' Cleo confided, wondering what he was getting at and why in his estimation she would have put herself through such a humiliating confrontation.

'Didn't it occur to you that *she* might have been

the liar?' Ari pressed with a frown of bemuse-
ment as he stared down at her, his extraordinary
eyes holding her full attention. 'Easy enough to
borrow a child to make such a visit on a rival and
see her off.'

Cleo blinked rapidly. 'I never thought of that…
I have to admit that that suspicion never once
crossed my mind—'

'You didn't do *anything* to check out her conten-
tion that she was living with him?' Ari stressed in
wonderment, and he shook his tousled dark head
slowly. 'You just condemned him out of hand on
her word. Maybe she was telling the truth, but
maybe she wasn't. Whichever, you should have
checked it out, not simply assumed that he was
guilty as charged. Please be a little more thorough
in your approach if I ever get on your wrong side.'

Cleo swallowed hard, taken aback by his very
different reading of the situation while seeing her
own skewed reasoning process at the time. Her
innate distrust of the opposite sex had fuelled her
willingness to believe that Dominic had been lying
to her and she had never given him the chance to
defend himself, which really hadn't been fair, she
belatedly acknowledged.

Ari's mobile phone rang as he was pulling on
his shorts. It was his London lawyer, a stuffy old-
fashioned sort of man, who tended to talk in a

confidential murmur and preferred face-to-face meetings to phone consultations, but he was very wily and knowledgeable, which was why Ari retained his services.

'I'll be back in London tomorrow,' Ari confirmed. 'What sort of news?'

Regrettably, the sort of news that Oliver Matthews didn't wish to discuss on the phone. Ari suppressed a groan and mastered his impatience as he agreed to see the lawyer the following afternoon.

'Oliver's being cagey as usual, which means that what he has to tell me is unlikely to be good.' Ari sighed, his lean, dark face shadowing as Cleo asked him what was happening. 'It can only relate to my sisters. *Thee mou*, surely one of them can't be deceased as well—not at their age!'

Cleo closed a hand over the clenched fist that betrayed his tension. 'I'm coming with you to see the lawyer,' she said soothingly. 'Don't be such a pessimist.'

CHAPTER NINE

'LUCY REMEMBERS YOU,' the caseworker commented.

'Thank goodness,' Cleo responded cheerfully. 'I was worried she would forget our faces after two weeks.'

Lucy was smiling widely at her, showing the tooth that had finally emerged during their absence and which had, apparently, given her foster carer some sleepless nights. She lifted her hand to Ari's jaw and giggled.

'He feels just like a hedgehog, doesn't he?' Cleo quipped, because they had come straight from the airport and Ari hadn't yet shaved. A shadow of dark stubble surrounded his wildly sensual mouth.

'But it's sexy,' Ari informed her with all-male confidence.

And Cleo smiled as widely at him as his niece did. She was hoping the lawyer had some encouraging news for him, rather than the kind of depressing information he had received about the brother

he had never met and now never would meet. Instead, he was hoping to raise his brother's child,
striving to make up for what he viewed as his late
father's neglect. Ari had a lot of heart. He mightn't
like to show the fact, but his search for his father's
second family was the proof of his compassion.

When they entered the senior lawyer's imposing
office, Cleo immediately saw that the older man
was disconcerted by her arrival with his client.

'Mrs Stefanos may—' he began tightly.

'Cleo and I have no secrets from each other,'
Ari imparted with scorching assurance.

Feeling embarrassed by the suspicion that she
was unwelcome at the consultation, Cleo took a
seat beside Ari, and only moments later she had to
battle to keep her face composed because the older
man plunged straight into the matter he wished to
discuss. Sadly, Cleo would very much have preferred *not* to be present once she realised what the
issue encompassed.

'A *paternity* claim?' Ari repeated in a flat tone
of emphasis in which no discernible emotional expression could have been read. 'From whom?'

Cleo had gone rigid in her seat, her spine straight,
her hands clasped tight on her lap, not a muscle
moving in her small face. She had insisted on accompanying Ari to the appointment and pride would
not allow her to show how distressed she was by the

very idea of another woman giving birth to Ari's first child.

They had discussed having children but had decided it would be a year or two before they did because, at present, Lucy had needs that could well demand a lot of time and attention and she had to be their priority. Furthermore, they needed to adjust to being Lucy's parents before they could consider extending the family. But that Ari could still become a father *without* Cleo had never once struck Cleo as even a possibility! And now she was deep in shock at the discovery that the sex life prior to his marriage, which Ari had dared to say was none of her business, was promising to impact on both their lives in a way neither of them could have foreseen.

She sat in silence while Ari and his lawyer discussed prenatal DNA testing and the necessity of obtaining the birth mother's agreement to the non-invasive procedure. It only required a cheek swab from Ari and a blood test for the expectant mother. Ari sounded so calm and yet she felt sick to the stomach! How could he be so *calm*? Had he suspected that there could be a potential pregnancy risk with some woman? Was he one of those men who could occasionally be careless with precautions? He had not been irresponsible with her. But how was she to know how he had behaved with other women in his bed? That thought made her feel even more nauseous and distanced from him because Cleo was now at a stage where she could not bear even to *think* of Ari having bedded other women, and now she was being faced with the prospect of having to deal with the evidence of that fact for the next twenty years.

Forget twenty years, she thought almost hysterically. Any child would be around and part of her life as well for the whole of their marriage and lives. Children grew up but they did not go away. Ari was very responsible. He would be a supportive father to *any* child that was *his*. Such devastating news was a huge and cruel blow to receive in the very first weeks of their marriage.

Ari glanced at Cleo by his side, registering that she had not said a single word since her arrival. But then what did he expect after such an announcement? A paternity claim, his first. He was in shock, striving to hide it because Cleo was silently freaking out and he did not want to encourage her to feel that way. But he knew that, no matter how careful any male was, there was always the risk that a baby could be conceived. But to have a baby with that *particular* woman? Ari gritted his teeth while acknowledging that thinking negative stuff about his potential baby's mother was a very bad idea. He needed to stay off that fence until he knew more.

'Ready?' Ari was standing, looking down at her with an enquiring gaze because the appointment was over.

Cleo blinked rapidly, struggling to come out of the turmoil of her anguished thoughts and her sense of betrayal, but it was a serious struggle to pull herself together again. Shock, panic and dismay were all pulling at her simultaneously. Her image of Ari with a child who was not hers clawed at her like salt scattered on an open wound…

Yet Lucy was not her child, she reminded herself, sanity attempting to intrude on her intense mental upheaval. But Lucy *was* different, she reasoned. Ari had not been involved with Lucy's mother and Cleo was as much in love with tiny smiley Lucy as Ari was. If only Ari had not been such an unrepentant man whore, she found herself thinking helplessly, angry resentment assailing her because suddenly her shiny new marriage no longer seemed half as appealing as it had only hours earlier.

Not that that mattered, Cleo conceded unhappily. She loved Ari, flaws and all, and she was growing to love Lucy as well, and no way could she consider walking away from either of them for good. At the same time, however, she felt that she had to have some space to come to terms with what she had just learned. As it was, she felt utterly trapped by undesirable circumstances that couldn't be changed. It was painful too to be forced to accept that, although she would suffer much from the development, she had no rights whatsoever in such a situation.

'Just say what you're thinking,' Ari urged in a raw undertone in the back of the limousine, stunned by Cleo's ongoing lack of either questions or comment about a development that had knocked him for six.

Nor did it help that the prospective mother was Galina Ivanova, who could quite correctly declare that he had refused to have anything more to do with her. Had the woman truly been chasing him in an effort to tell him that she had fallen pregnant? Had he so misread the situation *and* the woman involved that he had inadvertently put himself very much in the wrong? He was appalled by the suspicion and determined to play his every next step by the book.

Cleo swallowed hard and breathed in deep. 'I didn't sign up for this,' she mumbled bitterly, half under her breath.

'Neither did I, but we're married now. Difficult issues must be faced together and dealt with together,' Ari murmured with a cool distance that she was painfully aware of. 'Are you with me or against me on this?'

The silence stretched because Cleo truly didn't know how to respond to that question in the state she was in at that precise moment.

'In this instance, silence is not golden,' Ari said very drily.

'Who *is* this woman?' Cleo asked tightly, having to force the question past her lips because she knew that she didn't really want the answer. She didn't want any image inside her head, particularly when she was thinking that it could be one of the bitchy wedding guests.

Ari frowned in astonishment. 'You weren't listening to what Oliver told us?'

'I sort of zoned out,' Cleo admitted grudgingly.

'Galina Ivanova, the woman you let into my office on your first day…and I censured you for it,' Ari reminded her doggedly. 'It sounds as though that was, very much, my mistake.'

'That brunette?' Cleo was horrified because the woman had possibly been the most stunning woman Cleo had ever seen, with a mass of tumbling silky black hair, cut-glass cheekbones, huge sultry brown eyes and a slender figure straight out of a fashion magazine adorned with legs as long as rail tracks.

'Yes,' Ari confirmed. 'If her claim is true, I will have to make amends for having asked her to leave my office. I cannot risk being on poor terms with her now.'

'No…of course not,' Cleo muttered sickly, sick to the stomach at the prospect of his having an ongoing relationship with the woman and merely reaching a new high of misery at his explanation.

'It was only one night—' Ari gritted with startling abruptness.

Cleo jerked up a hand to silence any such recollections and directed a blazing glance of reproach at him. 'No, no details, *please*!' she slung back at him in condemnation.

'You are not handling this in an adult way,' Ari rebuked her.

'I wonder how adult you would feel were I to tell you that I was pregnant by another man a few weeks after we had married. That is the *nearest* approximation I can make to your current position,' Cleo framed bitterly.

'In no way would that be the same, but I would accept it because you are my wife. Such things happen, Cleo, whether we want them to or not. Sometimes, nature or fate is in control, not us. Anyone who has sex must recognise such contingencies,' he bit out in a savage undertone.

Contingencies—the same word the lawyer had used at one point, Cleo dimly recalled, nicely sidestepping all more personal and intimate references to the child that was to be born. She recognised that Ari was now furious with her, as though she were the one who had brought this nightmare down on them, and that infuriated her. But it also scared her because she knew she loved him, and she didn't want this child to fatally damage their relationship. He expected her to stand by him and she *would* stand by him because she loved him… but that didn't mean she had to *like* it.

Still in a state of passionately rejecting their plight, Cleo resolved to go home for a visit. A trip to Scotland made sense, she reasoned. Her mother would talk sense to her and calm her down, drag her out of the turbulent feelings and urges that she could not afford to direct at Ari.

She needed time away from him to deal with the situation and come to terms with their altered future. *Stand up and grow up*, she told herself irritably, thoroughly ashamed of the emotions she was drowning in. She was so jealous, so bitter at the concept of another woman carrying Ari's child, particularly a woman as very beautiful as Galina was. No normal woman, she consoled herself, would want a Galina on the sidelines of their life, particularly not as the mother of an all-important eldest child.

Ari would be in regular contact with Galina from now on. He would be looking after the mother of his child, being supportive…and how could she fault him for that? Wasn't that what a decent man was supposed to do? Step up and accept full responsibility? Do whatever was in his power to support the expectant mother?

Gripped by yet another wave of anguish, Cleo fled upstairs to their bedroom to pack an overnight bag. She didn't pack anything more than jeans and tops. She wanted to be anonymous.

Ari filled the doorway. 'What the hell are you doing?' he gritted incredulously.

'I'm going to visit Mum…only for a few days,' Cleo responded stiffly. 'I think it would be the best thing for us both to have some space from each other for a *little* while.'

'The first bump on the road that we hit, you abandon ship and run!' Ari slashed back at her furiously.

He was losing his English. He would never have mixed up clichés like that in a normal mood. His beautiful eyes were scorching gold with anger and her tummy flipped and the breath shortened in her throat, making her chest feel tight. 'It's not like that,' she argued vehemently. 'I have to have some time alone, but I'm coming back.'

'Bully for you!' Ari bit out angrily. 'That makes me feel a whole lot better!'

'I'll get the train—'

'No, you won't. You'll fly there,' Ari countered squarely. 'As my wife, you have security needs. When are you planning to return?'

'Just the rest of this week...back Sunday,' Cleo promised, thinking fast because they had a visit scheduled with Lucy only a day later.

Ari dealt her an angry fulminating appraisal. 'I don't agree with this tack. Walking away doesn't deal with this... It's *running* away,' he condemned.

'No, it's not,' Cleo protested, turning away from the disturbing image of him in the doorway, all lean and dark and beautiful and absolutely everything that she loved. Tears prickled her eyes in a stinging lash. She didn't want to go, but she didn't want to stay either and say the wrong things, and she was terribly afraid that, in the resentful frame of mind she was in, she would totally say the *wrong* things to him. And he definitely did not deserve that, she reckoned wretchedly.

Nothing more was said. Cleo went to the airport, climbed on board the jet for the short flight and worked at drying the tears trickling down her face. She felt betrayed...but was that *his* fault? Or the fault of her ingrained habit of distrusting men? She supposed it had begun when her mother first poisoned her view of her father and had settled in hard after her infatuation with Dominic had been destroyed by his seeming lies. But then Ari had come along, and Ari was very honest and just about perfect, she reflected miserably. He hadn't pretended that he had fallen miraculously in love with her. He had asked her to marry him for Lucy's benefit. That was a praiseworthy act for his niece's welfare, but it was also an act and a level of honesty that increasingly cut Cleo to the quick. Loving Ari had made her more sensitive.

How did one trust a man with a woman like Galina when he didn't love his wife? Galina was ten times more beautiful and sexier than Cleo would ever be, and once she had Ari's child, she would have magnetic appeal for him. Cleo knew that. Ari set a deep value on blood ties and he would be very keen to spend time with his child. Only witness what he was willing to do for his half-brother's daughter! What might he wish to do for his *own* child with Galina? Wasn't there a very strong chance that what had initially attracted him to Galina would revive once he saw her with his child? And wouldn't it make sense that he could want to eventually marry Galina for the sake of his own flesh and blood?

And where would Cleo be then? His *practical* choice? Not the woman he loved, who could at least have felt secure in that love at such a testing time. Cleo didn't have that stability, that sense of safety, to ground her in their relationship. As a result, that first bump in the road that he had mentioned had been a complete car crash for her...

'Cleo...nothing's perfect.' Lisa Brown sighed at the kitchen island of the house attached to the pub that she and Cleo's stepfather ran. 'Not life, not people, not marriage. You can't blame Ari because he burst your fantasy bubble... He's right. These things do happen, whether we want them to or not. I thought you loved him—'

'I do!' Cleo proclaimed uncomfortably.

'Then why are you here with me?' the older woman prompted gently. 'He must be upset about this as well and you have to sort this out with him. Can you live with this child being a part of your life as well? It's that basic.'

'Maybe the DNA test will reveal that it isn't his kid,' Cleo opined, looking hopeful.

'Do you have cause to suspect that it may not be his?'

'No. I don't know anything about the woman, don't want to either!' Cleo confided in a distressed rush of honesty.

'In this scenario, you can't afford to take that attitude.' Lisa sighed. 'If you can't learn to cope with this, it could mean the end of your marriage—'

In receipt of that warning, Cleo lost colour. 'I don't want that.'

'Learn to cope with it, then,' her mother advised ruefully, sliding off her bar stool. 'Sorry, love, I have to get back to work.'

'That's fine. Just forget I'm here,' Cleo urged guiltily.

It was Sunday and she was due to fly home that evening. She had had several days and several sleepless nights to think stuff through. The blinding resentment, anger and turmoil *had* receded somewhat, leaving her facing the reality that she had to handle the situation as it was, not as she wished it could be. Pessimism had already convinced her that, of course, the baby would prove to be a Stefanos baby.

The doorbell buzzed and she slid off her stool, glimpsing her reflection in the hall mirror as she passed and grimacing because she hadn't bothered to put on any make-up and she was wearing 'comfort' clothes from her teenage years that consisted of a pair of lounge pants, a stretched, already over-sized pullover and slippers.

To say that she was shattered to open the door and find Ari standing there would have been an understatement. One glimpse of his familiar tall, lean and powerful figure and a complex tumble of emotions washed over her. Joy, consternation and annoyance that he had taken her by surprise and found her clad in her rattiest, oldest clothes.

'Ari…' she whispered shakily once she had found her voice again.

'We have some serious talking to do,' Ari intoned coolly, his gaze raking over every inch of her, noting the tender valley of smooth skin visible at the neck of her jersey, the curve of her hip as she turned towards him, blue eyes widening, golden curls tangled.

And both that announcement in that tone and the forbidding expression on his lean, darkly handsome features made Cleo's heart sink to her very toes.

CHAPTER TEN

'WE'LL TAKE THIS discussion to the hotel I'm staying in locally,' Ari decreed.

'I'm not going anywhere dressed like this.' Cleo sighed. 'Give me twenty minutes to change.'

His beautifully moulded mouth firmed. 'I'll wait in the car.'

Cleo fled back to the bedroom she had been using and stripped at the speed of a maniac before rushing into the shower. The whole time her brain was crackling with frantic frightened thoughts. Perhaps Ari had already decided that a divorce was the best way forward. Would he risk such a move in the midst of their application to foster Lucy? Or was it possible that the news of the baby that had been conceived with Galina could now take precedence over his niece? She supposed anything could be possible because she had run away rather than talk about that baby with him. Shame filled her as she frantically dried her hair and dabbed on some make-up to conceal her reddened eyelids. She *had* run home like a little girl rather than stand her ground and act like a grown woman, she conceded in mortification.

Clad in jeans, a stylish red top and sneakers, Cleo walked out to the car with her heart pounding very fast in her chest.

'I wasn't expecting you,' she admitted, filling the silence when she joined him.

Ari said nothing. A fierce rage had settled inside him as the days of her absence crept past on leaden feet. He couldn't initially credit that Cleo had run home to her mother until common sense kicked in and he contrived to imagine how he might have reacted to such a situation at her age. His bride was still very young, and if she did not have his life experience and greater maturity, that rested on *his* shoulders, because he had married her, hadn't he? In any case, none of that mattered when he was so hopelessly relieved to be back with Cleo again. At that moment nothing else really seemed to matter.

Predictably, Ari was staying at a madly grand country-house hotel with turrets, luxury suites and awesome service. Too twitchy to stand still or sit down, Cleo crossed the vast reception room with its ornate antique furniture and elaborate curtains and stood at one of the windows, which overlooked an immaculately kept lawn and trees. Ari offered her a drink and she asked for water.

As he slotted the glass between her fingers, she glanced up at him mutinously. 'I *was* planning to catch that flight tonight and come back to London,' she told him squarely.

'I wasn't prepared to wait that long,' Ari parried without skipping a beat.

The gleam of his dark golden eyes below curling black lashes ensnared her and the heat rose in her pale cheeks. 'I shouldn't have left in the first place,' she muttered reluctantly. 'But I... I just didn't know how to handle it—'

Ari lifted a straight ebony brow in challenge. 'And you think that *I* did?'

Cleo reddened even more, her discomfiture pronounced.

'I was as shocked by the information as you were,' he admitted quietly. 'But it also bothers me to see a pattern in your behaviour...'

Her brow indented as she shifted from one foot to the other. 'What pattern?'

'It worries me that we're in conflict again over a past that I cannot change,' Ari confessed levelly. 'We had an argument on our wedding day about my exes—'

'Not about their existence,' Cleo disagreed, lifting her head high. 'About you inviting them all to our wedding! As for this baby—'

'I had a normal sex life in which I took every possible precaution to ensure that there were no accidental conceptions,' Ari slotted in, his lean, darkly handsome face grave. 'No male can do more than that. Yet I feel that you are *blaming* me—'

'That's…that's just human nature in a tight and unpleasant corner,' Cleo protested uncomfortably, taking his point but not admitting the fact. 'And our wedding did make it rather obvious that your… er…past is rather extensive in comparison to mine.'

'Unfortunately for me, I didn't appreciate that I would end up married to a woman who would find my past so distasteful,' Ari breathed harshly.

'That's not fair. I'm not judging you. In fact, I would never have thought about your past sex life at all had it not been for all those women at our wedding,' Cleo pointed out truthfully, standing her ground. 'You're the one who put a spotlight on your past for my benefit.'

Ari felt rather less certain of his position than he had once been. A married friend had remarked after the wedding on *his* wife's comments concerning that inconsiderate guest list. He had shot himself in the foot, Ari recognised, owning his mistake but typically reluctant to acknowledge it.

'I'm not remotely concerned about your past history with other women unless it impinges on our marriage,' Cleo declared steadily, meeting his gorgeous eyes calmly. 'And sadly, this baby does, and it threw me for a loop, I'm afraid. You need to try and view this development from my point of view—'

'I have—'

'No, you haven't,' Cleo responded, with bitter certainty in that accusation. 'This isn't a *real* marriage, not the way others are. You married me for Lucy's sake. I don't have the security of knowing that you love me, so I felt more threatened than many women would by the idea of a former lover having your child and the constant contact between you that will obviously follow on from that continuing relationship.'

'I'm possibly not the most emotionally intelligent guy you will ever meet,' Ari breathed tautly. 'Well, we already know that from the wedding guest list…but I'm not totally stupid. When I wake up in the morning and you're not there and I miss you. Well, that's never happened to me before with a woman—'

'You missed me?' Cleo slotted in brightly.

'And I'm not used either to thinking about a woman all day, because that *seriously* interferes with my concentration, but I can't get you out of my head,' Ari complained. 'I look at you, and as far as I'm concerned, you're the most beautiful and sexy woman in the world, which means that I truly don't see anyone but you now…'

By that stage, Cleo was simply staring back at him in shock at that unexpected rambling speech.

Ari sent her a wolfish smile of achievement. 'I believe it's called love. So, yes, you do have the security of knowing that I love you and that, as far as I'm concerned, this is a *very* real marriage.'

Not quite able to jump that fast from her assumptions to what appeared to be her new reality, Cleo trembled and frowned. 'Do you mean that?'

'Hey, I'm the guy who couldn't wait until tonight to see you,' Ari pointed out without hesitation. 'And no, I don't know when exactly I fell in love with you or how it happened in the first place. I only know that we forged bonds at the very beginning that first night, and the minute I had you in my bed, I wanted you back there again in the worst way. And absolutely nobody else would do as a substitute.'

'Is that so?' Cleo queried as she finally shook free of her paralysis with the craziest, fiercest happiness circulating through her in an enervating surge. Nothing at all mattered at that moment but that he loved her. Everything else, she thought warmly, would just fall naturally into place. She was no longer second-best, no longer the practical choice of wife. In fact, she found herself suspecting that Ari would have married her anyway once he understood how he felt about her.

'That is so,' Ari confirmed, resting both hands on her slight shoulders, flexing possessive fingers over her fine bones, dark golden eyes aglow with more emotion than she had ever hoped to see there.

'Well, you were way behind me,' Cleo informed him teasingly. 'The first time I laid eyes on you, I wanted you. That's how I ended up in bed with you that first time. You were my fantasy.'

'I like being your fantasy, *kardia mou*. But I did notice you from the start. I thought it was because your clothes were too colourful for me,' he admitted. 'Only I think it was because you were so different from my usual type…and now I only have one type and it's you.'

'I like that,' Cleo confided sunnily. 'You do realise that I fell for you on our honeymoon?'

'I was ahead of you there,' Ari asserted with pride. 'I knew when you walked down the aisle towards me in the church. You looked magical and I was so excited that you were mine.'

Cleo frowned. 'But you never said that you loved me!' she censured.

'I'd made all those speeches about Lucy, and changing tack that fast made me feel a little lame,' he explained. 'But the way I was behaving, I think you should have guessed how I felt about you. I was jealous of every man that looked at you, possessive beyond reason, and I couldn't get enough of you in bed or out of it. If that's not love, what is?'

Cleo rested tender fingers against his hard jawline. 'I do love you very much and I'm so sorry I ran away. I always knew I was coming back, though—I should get points for that, shouldn't I?'

'I was worried you wouldn't come back,' Ari confessed in a driven undertone as he closed both strong arms round her and literally lifted her into close contact with his lean, powerful body. 'Do you think I didn't appreciate that that news from Galina Ivanova was a body blow?'

'I don't have much to say about that yet,' Cleo admitted honestly. 'I'll get used to the idea, though. Time will help—'

Ari froze and looked down at her with a sudden grimace. 'It's *not* my baby she's carrying,' he told her bluntly.

'*Not* your baby?' Cleo whispered in shock.

'No. The DNA test proved that the child isn't mine. I think I was the richest bet Galina had and she just hoped that I would turn out to be the father, but obviously I wasn't her only lover at the time—'

'You should've told me it wasn't your child

first!' Cleo exclaimed in rampant disbelief at that oversight.

'No. I wanted to wait. I needed to know that you were willing to accept me as I am, flaws and all… because it *could've* been my kid. I'm very grateful that it's not. It's not how I would want to have my first child, but if it had been mine, I would have stood by her, and that would have been a major challenge because I don't like her—'

Her brow furrowed. 'You don't like her?'

'Not when she was behaving like a stalker. She was a little weird with me,' he confided, his mouth tightening. 'I was with her once and never again. Then she began constantly phoning, turning up places I went, showing up at the office uninvited. It was all too much.'

'But you're safe now from those kinds of mistakes,' Cleo said with a wicked grin. 'I won't let you out of my sight very often. You are truly off the market now, Mr Stefanos.'

'Is that supposed to be a threat?' Ari husked, running his hands up below her top and levering it off her with the slick skill that only he could contrive. Her bra followed. He lifted his hands to cup her ripe curves and backed her towards the bedroom next door. 'Right now, seeing more of you feels more like a very exciting promise.'

With thrilling impatience, he bent down and

swept her up into his arms to carry her into the bedroom and lay her down on the wide, comfortable bed. Clothes were tossed aside and silence fell, broken only by little moans and mutters as they made love, satisfying the gnawing sense of insecurity that had attacked them both when they were apart. In the aftermath of all that excitement, Cleo lay in the circle of Ari's arms, feeling gloriously content and safe at last.

'I wanted my baby to be your first child. I suppose that was sort of childish and mean,' she conceded ruefully.

'I don't think so. I wanted the same thing, but I also knew that, even if you stood by me, it would damage our relationship. How could a child with another woman do anything else when we were so newly married?' Ari murmured grimly, his arms tightening their hold on her slight body. 'We'll go and pack your clothes and catch up with your mother. Since I assume you told her about the baby that isn't mine, we'll have to explain that it was simply a con. And when we get back to London tomorrow morning, I have a surprise for you…'

'What sort of a surprise?' Cleo prompted, twisting her head to look at him, loving those gorgeous tawny eyes of his.

'Something unexpected. It's up to you to decide

whether it's a positive or negative development,' he framed mysteriously.

'I don't like mysteries.'

'It won't be a mystery for long.' Ari ran a soothing hand down over her spine and grabbed her to kiss her again, and all thought of the surprise vanished under the sensual onslaught of his mouth on hers.

On the flight back to London the next day, he explained that her father had seen a picture of their wedding in a newspaper and had contacted him to ask if they could meet.

'I told him that you were away and I suggested we meet for coffee,' Ari explained. 'You may think that was interfering of me, but I wanted to *vet* him for you lest he was only getting in touch because you had married a rich man.'

In shock, Cleo gazed back at him. 'My father?' she gasped. 'Why would he get in touch?'

'Because he would like the chance to get to know you. He parted from the woman he was originally with several years ago and tried to track you down then. He was unable to find you because of course your mother has moved on, married and changed her name. He is in regular contact with the son and daughter he has and he has now told them about you. He seems pleasant enough and genuine in his interest in you and a little nervous as to his reception with you,' Ari told her levelly. 'But it's up to you what you choose to do.'

'Do we look alike?' Cleo demanded curiously.

'You're almost a doppelganger for your mother,' he reminded her with amusement. 'But you do definitely have your father's big wide smile. Would it bother your mother if you had contact with him?'

'No. He's old history, as far as she's concerned.'

Cleo smiled sunnily and looked at Ari. 'I will see him. Our contact may not amount to anything more than a couple of meetings, but I would like the chance to get to know him. It's a chance I never thought I'd have.'

'As long as it doesn't cause you distress,' Ari commented, his protectiveness touching her heart. 'You've got by without him all these years and I don't want you upset.'

'I've got you now…and hopefully Lucy some day soon,' Cleo pointed out gently. 'My world is a secure one. I'm very curious about my half-brother and sister as well. I would like the opportunity to meet them if…if I like him and, of course, if they want to meet me. Now that we're all grown up, it doesn't seem as controversial as it seemed when I was a teenager.'

'It struck me the very first time we met that we had a lot in common.' Ari curved her into his

arms as the limo wafted them through the traffic
on their homeward journey. 'And it really is a challenge to keep my hands off you...'

'*So* romantic, Ari,' she whispered cheekily.

'I've organised a special dinner for your home-
coming,' he announced with a smile of pure one-
upmanship. 'And a gift.'

'And you're such a trier,' Cleo pronounced with
a helpless giggle and sheer joy bubbling up through
her. 'Always determined to take top billing...'

EPILOGUE

Two years after that conversation took place, Cleo was on the island of Spinos in Greece. It was summer and a bunch of young children were playing a noisy game on the grassy space in front of the terrace where Cleo was enjoying tea with her mother.

'I love staying at the resort. Tell Ari thanks,' Lisa said happily. 'You know he won't let me thank him for all the free luxury holidays we get here.'

'We enjoy the company,' Cleo responded lightly, and it was true. Her stepfamily were lively company for her own little family and she got to enjoy spending time with her mother at the same time.

Lisa snorted with laughter. 'Like you couldn't find company with this place and Ari behind you! You're living the dream, my love. You and those babies of yours are going to have a wonderful life.'

'I certainly hope so.' Cleo contemplated the

huge mound of her pregnant tummy, being at that stage of pregnancy where she could no longer see her feet and when she felt as though she had been pregnant for ever, rather than a mere seven months.

She was carrying twins: two little boys she couldn't wait to meet. And considering the fuss she had made about the unplanned conception Ari's ex had tried to lay at his door, she did not have a leg to stand on when it came to her own. They had decided to wait for two years before starting a family, and then, over a year into their marriage, they had had a romp late one hot night in the swimming pool when Cleo had been ready to expire from the heat and… *Boom.* Cleo had conceived and twins were on their way, with Ari claiming that he was delighted, regardless of that conception having been an accident.

Ari might continue to insist that he hadn't changed, but he had definitely mellowed. His wardrobe was no longer colour-coded, and he had learned to live with the clutter of a toddler's life, not to mention a wife who was infinitely less organised and tidy than he was, Cleo reflected fondly.

And having observed her husband with Lucy, who was almost three years old now, for they had picked her birthday as the date she had been found and rescued, Cleo was pretty sure Ari *was* delighted about the little boys soon to join their family. He was brilliant with Lucy, who had recovered from her poor start in life slowly, reaching the milestones other children took for granted at her own pace. Luckily for her, Lucy had no lingering medical issues. Now she was a happy, healthy toddler with a shock of black hair and she still had Ari's eyes, except hers were full of mischief most of the time. Those dancing dark eyes full of love and trust had walked so easily into Cleo's and Ari's hearts. Lucy had finally become officially their adoptive daughter only a couple of months earlier, but they had become her foster parents within a few months of that first meeting.

Now watching Lucy walk up from the beach with her little fingers possessively clinging to the leg of Ari's denim shorts, Cleo smiled because father and daughter, uncle and niece, however you wanted to look at them, were very close. And Lucy couldn't wait for the babies to come, the little brothers she would undoubtedly fuss over and boss around.

'It's idyllic here,' her mother sighed happily.

She watched Ari come to a halt to answer his mobile phone. Lucy abandoned him and ran up to the house, ducking the other children, who were all older than her, and rushing up the steps to Cleo to climb straight onto her lap. Unfortunately, it was a lap no longer in existence since pregnancy had altered Cleo's shape, and she sat up to accommodate the little girl more comfortably.

'Sleepy,' Lucy grumbled, slotting her thumb into her mouth.

'I'll take you upstairs for a nap,' Cleo promised.

'Love you, Mum-mum,' Lucy sighed.

Cleo's mother stood up and lifted the little girl. 'I'll take her up. You're supposed to be staying off your feet in the afternoon,' she reminded her daughter as Lucy snuggled her head into her grandmother's shoulder. 'And I'll be a while. I like reading her a story.'

'I only do that at night.'

'Well, when Granny's here, it's naps as well,' Lisa said cheerfully.

'Thanks, Mum,' Cleo murmured, thinking about how grateful she had been for her mother's laidback attitude towards her getting to know her long-lost father.

Gregory Stevens was not the selfish, uncaring man Cleo had once imagined he would be. She saw her father when she was in London and she liked him, although she doubted that they would ever develop a truly close relationship. She had also met her half-brother, Peter, who was a medical student and very down to earth. Her half-sister,

Gwen, hadn't yet agreed to meet up with Cleo and clearly wasn't sure she wanted the connection, and that was fine with Cleo. She had no desire to upset anybody and thought it was sad that Gwen's loyalty to her mother should have made meeting Cleo contentious. But Cleo was so happy in her own life that she had no need to put pressure on anyone.

Ari, having been cornered to settle a dispute in the kids' ball game, mounted the steps into the shade. He scrutinised Cleo, lying there all golden and ripe and so damned sexy it made him smile, because he knew that if he told her she looked like some sensual fertility goddess in her current condition, she would threaten to slap him. Unlike her husband, Cleo was way *past* finding pregnancy sexy.

He sat down in the seat his mother-in-law had vacated. 'Oliver's got information on the whereabouts of Lucas's twin sister,' he told her in an excited surge, his gorgeous dark eyes golden and bright with satisfaction, for he had been chasing dead ends in his search for his siblings for the whole of their marriage.

Cleo sat up. 'No bad news?' she checked.

'Well, Oliver said it's a mix. She's healthy, not an addict or anything like that. Clever girl, has a business degree, but, as Oliver put it and, no, I don't know what he means by it, she's had a lot of bad luck.'

'Oh, dear… You'll have to be careful about how you deal with her,' Cleo warned him. 'No bull-in-the-china-shop approach. You've seen how differently my siblings have reacted, so you have to accept that you may not be a welcome arrival in her life.'

Ari raised a cynical ebony brow and said drily, 'Beware Greeks offering you a small fortune?'

'Ari! There's much more to it than the bottom line of an inheritance!' Cleo framed worriedly, fearful that he would be tactless and would destroy the potential relationship before he even got the opportunity to have one.

Ari just laughed, all sun-bronzed and gorgeous and smiling, his spectacular eyes glittering. 'I was only teasing you. I'll find out what Oliver has to tell me about her "bad luck".' His handsome mouth took on a sardonic twist at that phrase. 'And I will act accordingly, but you have no idea how relieved I am just to find her and know she's alive and healthy.'

'I do understand,' Cleo protested, linking her fingers with his to tug him down to her. 'Now, just one kiss…'

'Just one kiss could lead to more,' Ari warned her thickly, leaning down, closing his beautifully moulded mouth to hers and saying huskily, 'Do you have any idea how much I love you?'

'Possibly just as much as I love you,' Cleo whispered as she gave herself up to that passionate kiss.

* * * * *

Couldn't put
Promoted to the Greek's Wife
down? Don't miss the next instalment in
The Stefanos Legacy trilogy,
coming soon.

Why not also dive into these other
Lynne Graham stories?

Christmas Babies for the Italian
The Greek's Convenient Cinderella
Cinderella's Desert Baby Bombshell
Her Best Kept Royal Secret
The Ring the Spaniard Gave Her

Available now!

#3985 BOUND BY HER RIVAL'S BABY
Ghana's Most Eligible Billionaires
by Maya Blake

Why, wonders Amelie, does she feel such a wild attraction to Atu? He wants to buy her family's beach resort, so he's completely off-limits. Yet surrendering to their heat was inevitable...and now she's pregnant with his heir!

#3986 THE ITALIAN'S RUNAWAY CINDERELLA
by Louise Fuller

Talitha's disappearance from his life has haunted billionaire Dante. Now he'll put their relationship on fresh footing—by hiring her to work for him. Yet with their chemistry as hot as ever, will he ever be able to let her go again?

#3987 FORBIDDEN TO THE POWERFUL GREEK
Cinderellas of Convenience
by Carol Marinelli

The secret to Galen's success is his laser-sharp focus. And young widow Roula is disruption personified! Most disruptive of all? The smoldering attraction he can't act on when he hires her as his temporary assistant!

#3988 CONSEQUENCES OF THEIR WEDDING CHARADE
by Cathy Williams

Jess doesn't know what she was thinking striking a just-for-show arrangement to accompany notorious playboy Curtis to an A-List wedding. What will the paparazzi uncover first—their charade...or that Jess is now expecting his baby?

#3989 THE BILLIONAIRE'S LAST-MINUTE MARRIAGE
The Greeks' Race to the Altar
by Amanda Cinelli
With his first bride stolen at the altar, Greek CEO Xander needs a replacement, fast! Only his secretary Pandora—the woman he holds responsible for ruining his wedding day—will do... But her touch sparks unforeseen desire!

#3990 THE INNOCENT'S ONE-NIGHT PROPOSAL
by Jackie Ashenden
After everything cynical Castor has witnessed, there's almost nothing he's surprised by. But naive Glory's offer to sell him her virginity floors him! Of course, it's out of the question. Instead, he makes a counter-proposal: become his convenient bride!

#3991 THE COST OF THEIR ROYAL FLING
Princesses by Royal Decree
by Lucy Monroe
Prince Dimitri's mission to discover who's leaking palace secrets leads him to an incendiary fling with Jenna. As their connection deepens, could the truth cost him the only woman that sees beyond his royal title?

#3992 A DEAL FOR THE TYCOON'S DIAMONDS
The Infamous Cabrera Brothers
by Emmy Grayson
Anna has spent years healing from her former best friend Antonio's rejection. Then a dramatic fall into the billionaire's arms spark headlines. And his solution to refocus the unwanted attention? A ruse of a romance!

YOU CAN FIND MORE INFORMATION ON UPCOMING HARLEQUIN TITLES, FREE EXCERPTS AND MORE AT HARLEQUIN.COM.

HPCNMRB0122B

*Why, Amelie wonders, does she feel such a wild attraction
to Atu? He wants to buy her family's beach resort, so he's
completely off-limits. Yet surrendering to their heat was
inevitable…and now she's pregnant with his heir!*

*Read on for a sneak preview of
Maya Blake's next story for Harlequin Presents*
Bound by Her Rival's Baby

A breeze washed over Amelie and she shivered.

Within one moment and the next, Atu was shrugging off his
shirt.

"Wh-what are you doing?" she blurted as he came toward her.

Another mirthless twist of his lips. "You may deem me an
enemy, but I don't want you catching cold and falling ill. Or
worse."

She aimed a glare his way. "Not until I've signed on whatever
dotted line you're determined to foist on me, you mean?"

That look of fury returned. This time accompanied by a flash
of disappointment. As if he had the right to such a lofty emotion
where she was concerned. She wanted, no, *needed* to refuse this
small offer of comfort.

To return to her room and come up with a definite plan that
removed him from her life for good.

So why was she drawing the flaps of his shirt closer? Her fingers
clinging to the warm cotton as if she'd never let it go?

She must have made a sound at the back of her throat, because
his head swung toward her, his eyes holding hers for an age before
he exhaled harshly.

His lips firmed and for a long stretch he didn't speak. "You need
to accept that I'm the best bet you have right now. There's no use
fighting. I'm going to win eventually. How soon depends entirely
on you."

The implacable conclusion sent icy shivers coursing through her. In that moment she regretted every moment of weakness. Regretted feeling bad for invoking that hint of disappointment in his eyes.

She had nothing to be ashamed of. Not when vanquishing her and her family was his sole, true purpose.

She snatched his shirt from her shoulders, crushing her body's instant insistence on its warmth as she tossed it back to him. "You should know by now that threats don't faze me. We're still here, still standing after all you and your family have done. So go ahead, do your worst."

Head held high, she whirled away from him. She made it only three steps before he captured her wrist. She spun around, intent on pushing him away.

But that ruthlessness was coupled with something else. Something hot and blazing and all-consuming in his eyes.

She belatedly read it as lust before he was tugging her closer, wrapping one hand around her waist and the other in her hair. "This stubborn determination is admirable. Hell, I'd go so far as to say it's a turn-on, because God knows I admire strong, willful women," he muttered, his lips a hairsbreadth from hers, "but fiery passion will only get you so far."

"And what are you going to do about it?" she taunted a little too breathlessly. Every cell in her body traitorously strained toward him, yearning for things she knew she shouldn't want but desperately needed anyway.

He froze, then with a strangled sound leaving his throat, he slammed his lips onto hers.

He kissed her like he was starved for it. *For her.*

Don't miss
Bound by Her Rival's Baby,
available March 2022 wherever
Harlequin Presents books and ebooks are sold.

Harlequin.com

HARLEQUIN

Heartfelt or thrilling, passionate or uplifting—Harlequin is more than just happily-ever-after.

With twelve different series to choose from and new books available every month, you are sure to find stories that will move you, uplift you, inspire and delight you.